Tom Forrest's
COUNTRY CALENDAR

Tom Forrest's COUNTRY CALENDAR

Compiled from the original material
written for THE ARCHERS by
C. GORDON GLOVER
and
PHIL DRABBLE

British Broadcasting Corporation

Published by the British Broadcasting Corporation
35 Marylebone High Street, London W1M 4AA

ISBN 0 563 1741 10

First published 1978

Printed in England by Tonbridge Printers Ltd
Shipbourne Road Tonbridge Kent

Illustrations by Thomas Bewick
Cover shows Bob Arnold as Tom Forrest
Photograph by Michael Hopkinson

Preface

For over twenty-five years the hour-long Sunday-morning broadcast of *The Archers* has been introduced by the rich authentic country voice of Tom Forrest, played for all that time by Bob Arnold, himself a Burford man, and it has been produced untiringly by Tony Shryane. Many writers have provided the material but of recent years it has been written by C. Gordon Glover, who died in 1975, and by Phil Drabble, the naturalist.

I have edited and rearranged these introductions, adding material of my own in an attempt to give a picture of the changing year, as well as more information about old country superstitions and weather lore, and hope the book will help to remind you not only of the countyside, but also of your many old friends in Ambridge.

Charles Lefeaux

January

If the grass grows in Janiveer
It grows the worse for all the year.

Good Morning!

One day over Christmas when it was pretty cold, Prue and I were turning out a cupboard and came across an old book, one of those they used to have in Victorian times, crammed full of all sorts of bits and pieces of information for every day in the year, and telling you things like how the months got their names and so on. We got very interested in this and I thought you might be too, so as we go along I'm going to tell you about the names of the months, and some of the other odd things we found in the book, as well as the things I usually talks to you about on a Sunday morning.

Well apparently, this month we're in now was dedicated by the Romans to their God Janus because he had two faces, so he could look back on the year that had gone and forward to the one to come. And reading that set me thinking of an old country rhyme I used to know:

The blackest month of all the year
It is the month of Janiveer.

And it is, isn't it? The wind can roar and whistle in the trees, and the sky can be grey, while the worms have dug deep down in the earth and the bats, hedgehogs and dormice are all asleep hibernating till the cold is over. Townsfolk don't always realise that when it's really cold in the country you can pick up a bucket and the handle can actually stick to the palm of your hand - that's how cold it can be.

Still, however hard the weather is, the days gradually begin to get longer and the first snowdrops soon begin to peep out in sheltered spots and the winter wheat can look beautiful - just like stripes of corduroy, as somebody said the other day, so I'm beginning to look forward to spring, spring to me always means robins. I'm sure you know the story of the 'Babes in the Wood'? Well then, who covered them with leaves to keep them warm? Cock Robin, of course. And that isn't as silly as it sounds because if you stop for as many breathers as I do when you're digging the garden, I bet it isn't long before a cheeky little robin comes to see what you're at, and I'm sure that if you went to sleep in a wood it wouldn't be long before one came to find out what that funny shape on the ground was. And if there was a breath of spring in the air or a glint of sun, you'd probably wake up to find one sitting on your chest carrying a beakful of soft moss or leaves. Some folk would say he was just building a nest but I'll wager that's what started the story of a robin covering the babes in the wood.

Robins are so trusting and friendly that country folk believe they must have a drop of God's blood in their veins and that if

you do one the slightest harm, you'll have dreadful luck for the rest of the year.

So if you like them as much as I do, you go and buy a few meal worms from your local pet shop and put them on the bird table when your robin is around. As soon as he discovers what they are, he'll give you no peace! 'My' robin - I call him mine because he's always hanging round our back door - he flies straight down, perches on my hand and takes the worms out of my fingers. It's much more exciting than keeping a canary or budgie, I can tell you!

Now the other night I was out in the woods and there wasn't a whisper of breeze. It was so quiet that even with a lifetime of practice I couldn't move around without hearing the twigs crack under my feet like cannons going off. So I kept still for a bit to listen if anyone else was cracklin' about and there wasn't a sound. Not a whisper - when suddenly there was an almighty scream from the clearing just over the hedge which made me jump and I could feel the hairs prickle up the back of me neck. But, well, I've been keeperin' for the best part of a lifetime so I knew what it was, and it wasn't really sinister at all. It was just a love song that every countryman hears at this time of year. It was a vixen letting any dog fox within earshot know that she was turned on in a big way, so what about a date? Then as I knew I should, I heard a dog fox reply from about half a mile away with three short sharp barks to tell her he'd heard - and that it seemed a good idea! Then another suitor joined in and the vixen called again to tell the world that it would soon be cubbing time again. Although her screams were probably ecstasy, they sounded mournful and unworldly to me and a good start for a real chilly ghost story, I'd say.

Now I'll tell you about something else I heard the other day. I was right down the wood in about the quietest part, just checking where the pheasants would be for the shoot, when I heard the tiniest twittering sound you could imagine. I knew what it was the moment I heard it because it was so high pitched that my ears could only just hear it. As you know, as you get older, your hearing gradually dulls at the top end of the scale, so that sounds you could hear as a lad are often inaudible after about the age of forty. Now this sound I heard was almost as high pitched as a bat, and it came from the very top of a stand of birch trees. I stood absolutely still - and then I saw a little bird flittering from twig to twig in the tree tops. Once I'd spotted him I soon saw his mates, a flock of twenty or thirty, working their way across the wood. They were goldcrests, the smallest British bird, even smaller than a Jenny Wren, and although they're not rare, they're uncommon enough to give me a thrill whenever I see them.

After a bit I heard another high-pitched note and could see ten or a dozen long-tailed tits feeding with the goldcrests. The tits were not much bigger in the body, but they had huge long tails, floating in the breeze behind them, so they looked like tiny helicopters doing aerobatics in the tree tops. It was just like watching an aerial fairy pantomime and the bonus for me was to discover that in spite of not being as young as I was, my hearing is still sharp enough to hear their chorus, and that pleased me no end.

When I was young we used to call our local gamekeeper Owd Velveteens. All keepers were called velveteens then because they used to wear velvet waistcoats. It was a sort of badge of office, you see. Only it wasn't really velvet of course. It was moleskin! In those days part of a keeper's job was to keep the moles down and there was only one way of doing that. They had to trap them, and it was such a skilful job that a nice moleskin waistcoat was a sort of status symbol.

Now where I was brought up, they used to call moles 'unts' and I think they still do in Shropshire, and a very descriptive word it is - unts! Actually it's a corruption of want, because moles are always so hungry they're always wanting more, like Oliver Twist. And we used to believe they starved if they were without food for more than an hour or so, but that's a bit of an exaggeration, though like most old country beliefs, it isn't so far out, for moles do feed and rest in shifts and when it's dark and the worms come out at night the moles often come out too and catch them. And of course that's dangerous for 'em because foxes hunt at night and so do owls. And herons catch a lot of moles at dawn and dusk - those'd be the greedy ones that came out too early or stopped up too late, I reckon.

Mind you, moles don't chase worms by digging after them as you might think. They dig their tunnels and the worms just drop into them. So do beetles and all sorts of grubs and insects too. So all the old mole has to do is to wander along his tunnels and pick up his dinner as he goes! The snag is they are very quarrelsome, moles are, and if they find another mole in their tunnel, they set about him so savegely that it's often a battle to the death. But at this time of year when the ground's waterlogged after all the rain we've had, moles work very close to the surface. Partly because that's where the worms are and partly because they'd be drowned if they went any deeper.

If you go for a drive round about now and look at a wood from the road you might think there's nothing deader. The leaves are off and the branches look lifeless, the bracken's turned from autumn gold to faded brown, and the grass is withered and brittle, and the water in Ambridge Hall lake looks as grey and cold and forbidding as you'd find it was if you dipped your hand in. In fact it's a depressing time of year to look at the country - from a distance. But you get out of your car - and come into the woods with me, and you'll soon change your mind! Nature's sometimes tough and uncomfortable but she's never depressing.

The snowdrops are coming out in our woods, and I know we're later than some parts, but down south or where it's sheltered, I expect the primroses are in bloom too by now, and the birch and hazel catkins are on the twigs with the promise that they'll swell into lambs' tails by the time the real lambs have been born and have got tails of their own to frisk with. And there's been an old cock blackbird carolling outside our bedroom window for some time. He was hesitant at first as if he was only tuning up but there's no doubt about it now. He means business - and it's not so much a lyric for his lady-love as a warning to rivals that they'd better not trespass on his territory! The rooks are back at the rookery, not actually nesting yet but staking their claims to the best trees, and in every mild spell at this time of year the hares start jacking, and sparring, and rehearsing their mad courtship dances of the early spring. These are all only little signs, clues you might say, of hopeful things to come. But they're there all right.

I love this time of year myself, whatever the weather. You see, lots of jobs in the country have to stop when the light goes. You can't prune trees in the dark, can you? Or go hedgin' or ditching, so we sometimes knock-off around four and it's lovely to sit by the fire with a good cup of tea and feel the warmth winkling out the stiffness of a long day's work in the open.

Visited all night by troops of stars.

But at night when there's a frost about what a glitter there is in the clear night skies - it makes you feel very small, doesn't it? I remember seeing a play in Borchester by some famous Irish writer once and one of the characters who was a bit drunk said quite sudden like, 'What *is* the stars?' And I sometimes wonder that - what *is* the stars? Of course I knows what the obvious ones look like and where they are - the Great Bear and the Little Bear, and the Pole Star sitting up there, due north. And those three bright ones in a row - Orion's Belt they call them - and beautiful they all are, ain't they? But those nights can be very cold, and then lots of little birds die just because their body area is too big for them to keep warm. Now, the wrens get over this by roosting all together, sometimes a dozen or twenty at a time. They creep into a crevice or a nesting box one after another until it's crammed to bursting and so manage to keep one another warm. But the cold can bring other dangers to some birds - woodpeckers for instance. If they go after insect larvae in the tunnels bored by beetles in trees, and the trees are frozen, they can die of frostbite of the tongue, and herons and kingfishers often die if the frosts last a long time. But the danger for birds like partridge, which roost - or 'jug' - on the ground, is surprise attack from predators. So the whole covey go into the centre of a field and sit all night in a group with their heads pointing outwards so nothing can creep up on them from behind - and that's clever, isn't it?

Full many a flower is born to blush unseen,
And waste its sweetness on the desert air.

Now it struck me the other day while I was talking to Dan in The Bull, as some of you as listens to our Ambridge stories must sometimes wonder - what about some of the other folks as lives in the village? Some we never hear of - what about them? Well there's an old bachelor fellow, name of Ben Todd - must be all of eighty years old. He's a very quiet old fellow but he does love to get talking about the old days when he was a man of steam traction and when the farmyards fairly hummed with the music of the threshing tackle. Well, it must be all of six months back when I dropped in one morning to have a beer in the Raven, a little pub in Darrington. There was just one old fellow in there, and he said, 'You be Tom Forrest from Ambridge, b'aint ye?' 'Yes,' says I. 'That's me.' 'Then tell me,' he says, 'Is old Ben Todd about? Still alive is he?' 'Yes,' I said, Ben Todd was about, and very much alive. 'Well,' says the old fellow, 'next time you sees him, tell him as how his old mate Corney Peters was asking after him. Great pals we was when we worked together on the old machines. Tell him as maybe I'll git over and see him one of these days.' Well, next Thursday I happened to see Ben. 'Saw a friend of yours the other day, Ben - name of Corney Peters.' 'You never did,' says Ben. 'Still alive, is he? Well Mr Forrest, next time as you sees Corney, tell him as maybe his old pal Ben Todd'll git over to see him one of these days.' And do you know, I suppose I've taken the same

message between these two old jokers half a dozen times in the past six months! Neither of them can believe as the other is still alive! As for either of them 'gitting over the see each other one of these days' ... well, it's too silly to be thought about...

Another day this week I was over Penny Hassett way round about sunset time, when all of a sudden a great cloud come across the red sky. It was starlings - hundreds of thousands of them going back to roost. Most of them foreigners from the Continent, and they wasn't there because we've joined the Common Market either! No, for hundreds of years come wintertime we've had these invasions from the colder parts of Europe and they out-numbers our native birds by millions. Now most folks hasn't got a good word to say for starlings. Come to that, nor did I a year or two back when thousands of them decided to make a real slum of one of the bits of woodland as I looked after; and I can tell you that there's nothing makes more of a mess in a coppice than winter starlings if they decides to take over, and it's the same in the cities when they flies back from a day's foraging in the countryside and settles down on the Town Hall for the night. But when the starlings is all together and in full flight - especially around sunset time - what a wonderful sight they makes, thousands of them flying as though they was a single bird. I pulled my truck off the road for a minute or two just to watch the show, as you might say. And a proper show it was as they made their patterns in the sky, wheeling and spiralling and cutting every kind of caper. But suddenly, the whole flock seemed to come at me flying low over the top of my truck. And then I heard it - the sound of those thousands of wings not twenty feet above my head - it was like a wind with feathers rushing through the sky. And then as though they was a single bird, the whole company was gone, heading for their roost right away over Penny Hassett. And after seeing that, I think I'll forgive them for all the row and the mess they make.

On Monday I had one of the rottenest jobs that's come my way for a long while. All that dry weather we had made lots of dead leaves, grass and bracken that blew into every ditch and hollow, and then in the wet autumn it all went soggy and settled in the drain bottoms. So this last week or so we've had a lot of blocked land drains and little pools started coming in the corners of fields and all sorts of places where they shouldn't be. George and Gordon and the farm chaps have been out trying to free them - but it's the sort of job you soon get sick of. So I decided the least I could do was to get out and pull my weight with them. Now good resolutions like that make you feel grand in the warmth of the bar at The Bull, but when the time comes to do them, it's another matter. I don't know if you've ever had to free a field drain but the first thing to do is to get a set of drain rods. You know, those bamboo poles about a yard long and as thick as your thumb. On each end of the rods there is a brass screw, so as each rod goes up the pipe you can screw another on, pushing them right up the drain pipe until you feel where it's blocked. Then you pull the rods out again and lay them on the top of the ground so you can see where to dig down to find the pipe that's blocked or broken. I said it was a rotten job. Well, your hands get cold enough when you shove the rods along the pipe but when you pull them out they go numb and when you do it again you get 'hotache' in your fingers till they feel as if they've been run over by a steam roller. There's no pain I know worse than hotache. As bad as toothache, I always think. Well I know some Clever Dicks'll say what I should have done is get stuck-in with a spade to warm myself up and then I wouldn't have had hotache, but all I can say is let'em come and try, because if there's a wetter, colder, dirtier job, I haven't met it yet!

As the day lengthens
So the cold strengthens.

January's a 'hungry' month for most of the birds and animals in our woods. Nothing much growing and most of the berries and seeds that fell in autumn eaten weeks ago. But you know there's some good housekeepers as never went to school or cookery classes. And I was watching a squirrel last back-end, collecting nuts. Shouldn't have, of course. A good keeper ought to shoot all squirrels as vermin. But we don't do everything right, do we? I did raise my gun but he was so beautiful I put it down again. Kidded myself I'd learn a bit more about his habits so I'd be more efficient next time. But the real reason was that I'm getting a bit soft and couldn't pull the trigger! The older you get, the less you like killing things. Anyroad, this squirrel, a grey one of course, was picking the nuts off hazel bushes, running about fifty yards into the wood with them, and then burying them in the leaf mould and I dug one up after he'd gone, to see how deep it was. I found it a couple of inches under the surface, quite hidden, and it made me wonder whether he really was a good housekeeper and knew where he'd stored it and would ever be able to find it again.

Well, I found the answer yesterday. I watched the same squirrel - or one just like him - searching for nuts just where I'd seen him bury them weeks before. He wasn't going straight to the spot, so he hadn't exactly remembered. But he seemed to know which area to look in. And he seemed to be hunting more by scent than memory because he hopped around and then he stopped as if he was listening. But he wasn't listening. He was sniffing. I suppose the nuts had ripened till they had a wonderful scent like good wine does. His nose savoured it like a connoisseur and then he dug down and got it out gently with as much delight as if it'd been vintage port he'd got.

He wasn't the only good housekeeper around either because I saw a woodmouse with a long tail and big brown eyes, storing acorns. She had a white waistcoat and golden fur on her back.

But what took my fancy was how she handled the acorns which were too big for her to hold. She spun them round and dribbled them where she wanted them just as neat as a footballer in the cup-tie.

I always think of the bottom end of January as being about the most dangerous time for birds and other wildlife and when there are hard frosts and snow it isn't difficult to visualise them starving and freezing to death.

And I don't know how it is with you but this year we don't seem to have nearly as many garden birds as usual. Normally the fat which Prue hangs outside the kitchen window is swarming with Tom Tits, stuffing themselves as if they hadn't eaten for weeks. She puts out apple peel and cores, and any fruit that goes a bit soggy on the bird table, and thrushes and blackbirds appear out of thin air to gobble down anything they can get.

But not this year. We've got less birds than I can ever remember. Now, the cause can't be the hard weather we've been having because there has been a shortage ever since autumn, long before the first frost came. So the disaster that hit them was not winter weather but the summer drought. Now I don't think it actually killed many birds. It just slowed down their breeding because they knew, instinctively, that there wouldn't be enough food to rear their young on. Thrushes and blackbirds, for instance, need hundreds of worms to feed their brood, and worms suffered terribly in the drought. Those which didn't die had to dig down deep where the birds couldn't reach them, and not only to escape, but to find moisture. And the shortage of worms hit many animals even harder than the birds. Badgers, for instance. About half the food they eat is worms, so there have been a lot of very thin weedy badger cubs about and hedgehogs have suffered too. But the funny thing is that foxes, which also eat lots of worms, seem to be in marvellous condition, so you never can tell with Nature, can you?

February

February fill the dyke
Either with the black or white.

And a proper wet, slushy and gloomy old month February often is too. You may wonder about the black and white in the old rhyme but, of course, the black is the rain and the white, the snow. And it may not be because February is so wet in itself but because the rains in December and January have made the land so sodden that the extra rain fills the dykes and ditches because it can't soak into the ground. Still the coltsfoot has been in flower for some time, there are lots of primroses about, and of course the crocuses are up. Did you know crocuses are dedicated to St Valentine? But I'll be telling you a bit more about him in a minute.

Now that old book I was telling you about says that for the Romans February was the month of purification, and it got its name from Februo, which for them meant 'To purify by sacrifice'.

Although it's often a very cold month some birds show the first signs of getting ready to nest. Mistle thrushes, which are about half as big again as song thrushes, take up their territories and choose their sites, and they often choose exposed ones which is very stupid of them because magpies, jays and carrion crows often steal all the early eggs well before they can hatch.

But back to St Valentine - you know his day is the fourteenth and in some ways for me that's the start of the New Year. You see it's the time when some things begin to look as good as new - there's been the early lambing, the hedges have been trimmed and cleaned, the rooks is setting up a rare old racket as they gets their nursery quarters ready, the sallows is turning purple and the willows is trailing their leaf-buds in the wind. My pheasants had always got a real cock-and-henny look about 'em by now as the shooting was over and on the south side of our woodland the other day I saw the first windflowers poking through. And, of course, the partridges is pairing like they's always been said to do St Valentine's Day.

Old Bill Shakespeare had a word or two to say about the 14 February - how does it go? Something like:

Good morrow, friends! St Valentine is past;
Begin these wood-birds but to couple now?

And I reckon that's about right, though in this funny old winter lots of 'em were at their love-making weeks ahead of schedule. Why, a pal of mine found a blackbird's nest with four eggs in it last day of January. But traditionally birds are supposed to pair and choose their mates on St Valentine's Day.

If there's a warm spell in the month, frogs and toads may wake up from their winter sleep and start moving towards small pools. Though, mark you, there aren't nearly as many of them about as there used to be, because farmers have filled in so many of their small ponds so they can plough the whole of their fields, and also because the spraying that is done to kill wireworm sometimes results in the insecticide poisoning ditches and pools if there's a sudden storm before the stuff has dispersed.

Now you might not think it, but every wood has warm and cold patches in it. When you walk round on a still summer evening there are always clouds of midges dancing in the same spots, and if you walk through in winter, some parts are beautifully warm and sheltered but others as cold as charity. There don't seem to be no rhyme nor reason about it and if I went into a strange wood I couldn't tell you where the sheltered spots would be likely to be. But pheasants know and generations of pheasants will choose the same branches to roost on. I always used to have the frost pockets marked on a big map in the estate office because it would have been a waste of time putting food plants there for them, because the flowers would soon have got nipped in the bud, so there wouldn't have been any berries.

Although Mr Woolley's shooting is no longer my responsibility, and of course 1 February is the end of the season, still I can't get a lifetime's habits out of my system, so I had a walk round the other day to jog my memory of hopes and fears realised. There was one day for instance, when a very important guest was invited, so George and I worked out exactly where to put him so he'd have the lion's share of the shooting and when the birds started to come over we were delighted. Everything went according to plan and we could see them streaming over 'Mr Big' and we congratulated ourselves on how clever we'd been. But talk about counting your chickens before they hatch! He had twenty-seven shots at the first stand - and never touched a feather. And the rest of the day was the same, and he made a proper fool of himself, so he didn't enjoy a moment of it. And that's a serious thing from a keeper's point of view, because our efficiency is judged partly on the size of the bag and when the season's over the bosses look back and say 'We didn't have many that day'. They forget it was them as couldn't hit 'em, and blame the keeper for not showing the birds, so it's all our fault, you see!

Do you know there's something odd about this time of year? One night last week, round about nine o'clock in the evening it was, my Prue suddenly said 'Hear that, Tom? There they goes out in the meadow - just hark at them.' 'Hark at what?' says I. And then I hears it right enough, such a carry on caterwauling, squalling and spitting as ever I heard. 'Cats' month again,' says Prue. 'No peace of a night-time!'

And right enough she is - 'Cats' month', that's what a lot of country folk calls February, for there's no doubt about it as there's spring-in-the-air for the cats. All of a sudden, after half-sleeping the winter away by the fireside, they all seems to decide that it's time to get out and about and square up to any other old Tom as has got the spring fever and is 'watching all the girls go by' as that song had it a few years back.

And I can tell you as it's not only the old Tom cats as kicks up a row of a night time. Oh, dear me, no - the she-cats has got songs of their own as well if they don't fancy what's come a-courting of them.

They do say as there's cat people and dog people, but I'd say I was a bit of both, for there's something about old pussy cat as intrigues me. And I wonder if any of you what keeps a cat has noticed these moods as takes them come February. In the house they likes suddenly to get up high on things, like the tops of wardrobes and dressers, and such. They'll rush around the room in circles, then stop and stare at nothing - or whatever's the 'something' as cats do stare at. Then it's half-way up the curtains, a bit of claw-stropping on the settee, and '*Miaow,* what about a bit of supper before I goes outside to be part of "cats" month?'

Well that's enough about cats - let's talk about the weather, shall we? You see Prue and I always listen to the long range weather forecasts on the wireless but I don't take much notice of them. When it's fine here, it's often raining or foggy in Penny Hassett or Borchester so they're bound to be right with one or other. Or wrong with both of 'em.

So I look out for the countryman's signs for what it'll be. I taps the old barometer, and if it moves slowly, I look for a longish spell of whatever it says. And when I get out of doors, I look at the sky and if the clouds are in tight little ridges that's a mackerel sky, not long wet and not long dry. And I've got an old fir cone in the porch that I picked up years ago. It shuts up tight as a clam in fine weather and opens when it's going to rain. Don't ask me why! And a friend of mine says his does just the opposite but the only thing I can think of is that fir cones like to shed their seeds when the ground is nice and damp for germination and to do that they have to open.

But at this time of year when we expect bad weather, the old rhyme I like best and have many a laugh over, is:

Wind from the south brings bad weather,
Wind from the north brings wet and cold together,
Wind from the west brings rain,
Wind from the east sends it back again!

That's enough to cheer you up, isn't it? Who says we're not a lot of old pessimists?!

And talking of the weather we get visitors from towns who say how sorry they are for us country chaps because we have to look after stock, whether it's rain or shine, blizzard or fog. But I never really mind what the weather's like because it's always a challenge, and we do have one advantage over the chaps who live in the towns - we don't have to commute. Or very few of us do. And it's marvellous on a snowy morning to be living on the job. Much better to be able to roll out of bed, shovel a bit of snow from the door and start work, than to have to travel miles in a commuter queue hating all the other chaps, or stand for hours waiting for the bus!

And one thing I likes in the country is watching the steam rise from the cattle's breath when they are fed on a winter's morning - it's such a homely friendly thing. And there's no music like the crow of an old barnyard cockerel when the air is sharp with frost! Even when it's dank and wet, the squelch of wellies is comfortable because it reminds me of how when I was a kid we only had leather boots and it was a work of art rubbing warm dubbin up the seams to make them more or less watertight!

And do you know, I've never lost the habit I learned then of making a mental note of every footprint in the snow or mud. When we all wore boots, they had hobnails which left clues as clear as fingerprints because no two patterns were alike - even with wellies the tread wears and it isn't difficult to trace who's been there.

Have you noticed how if folks is feeling a bit down in the dumps, then like as not they'll blame it on the weather? 'It's too muggy - gets me down this sort of weather.' Or else, when the sun's shining bright and hot on a fine summer's day, then sure enough there's those all ready to start moaning about it - 'Can't stand the heat,' or 'What we need's a drop of rain to freshen things up.' No, there's no pleasing some folks whatever the weather's doing, and I don't have to tell you as farmers is the worst of the lot! Not as I blame them, for their whole livelihoods depends on it, and if you says to one of them as the wheat and the barley's coming along nicely, then depend on it there's root-crops as is hollering out for a downpour. And if the root-crops gets it, why, it's flattened the barley...! And so on. But somehow whatever the weather the harvest always comes home, doesn't it?

You may remember that last month I was telling you about foxes barking at night and that it wouldn't be long before it was cubbing time - well I know it seems an unlikely story at this time of year but last night I was listening to a song of spring and a lovesong of spring at that! It wasn't a nightingale that had got his seasons mixed, and it wasn't even our old blackbird thanking Prue for the last crumbs of the Christmas cake. In fact it wasn't a bird at all, it was a clique of foxes clicketting!

That's another word for flirting and foxes are terribly noisy and almost as careless of danger as mad March Hares at mating time. They're fond of barking at the moon - and it was full moon last night.

Anyhow I heard the bark of a fox. Wow-wow-wow he went. Or we always think it was a he, but I wouldn't stick my neck out by saying it wasn't a vixen, 'cos I'm not sure about translating their language although I've spent a lifetime amongst 'em. The two main sounds they make, and I heard both last night, are short sharp barks, usually two or three, and an unearthly scream that's the nearest thing to a ghost I've ever heard!

Now I've watched a fox screaming and I think it's a warning and I'm pretty sure the vixen screams in anger if the dog tries to get fresh before she feels like making love. And I've seen her scream as part of the courtship too, so perhaps it's not so much 'No' as 'Maybe'!

Last night I heard the barks coming from three directions so I think that must be some sort of rallying call - and then I heard this wild screaming, though I didn't know if it was a vixen keeping her boy-friends in their place or the boys shaping-up to warn their rivals off - really primitive it sounded though I can tell you.

You know, I always associate bats with warm summer evenings, don't you? Warm evenings when the midges are biting and it's a pleasure to welcome anything that will bite them back! And bats do just that. They live on flying insects, flies and moths and mosquitoes, and they work hard all the summer and autumn trying to put on a layer of fat to last them through the winter. And when they have they hibernate, they creep into crevices among the beams and rafters, hang themselves upside down, wrap their leathery wings about them, and go to sleep for the whole winter.

That's the theory anyhow, but it don't always work out in practice. You see when they hibernate, their body temperature sinks so low they literally hang between life and death, and most of the good blood settles around the heart which is the only part that keeps up a normal body temperature and their breathing slows down so much they sometimes only draw breath once in every three or four minutes. In cold winters they use up so little energy that their reserves last right through and they wake up in spring ready to take up their normal lives again. But if we get a mild winter, they don't get so cold and they use up more energy, and have to wake up in the middle to feed. Well, of course, there aren't the insects about in winter that there are in summer so they have to work harder and harder for less and less and lots of them are dead by springtime. So you see hard winters are often better for creatures that hibernate than mild ones are, so when you are cold and uncomfortable think of the bats which are sleeping it all away. And in about three months, the bottom end of March or early April, they'll come out in nice time to scoff the flies that would otherwise have bothered you. And forget all those old wives' tales about bats getting in your hair. They don't. They do nothing but good, bats do.

Where the wind is on Candlemas Day
There 'twill abide till the second of May

A week or two back Arkwright Hall lake froze over. Or at least it would have froze over if it hadn't been for the wild duck. You might not think that a few birds weighin' no more than two or three pounds apiece could make much difference to whether a lake got frozen solid or not. But they can! You see ducks can't perch up in trees, like pheasants out of the way of foxes - and a fox would as soon have wild duck for supper as he would have pheasant. So in the normal way ducks spend the night roosting out on the water or on the bank near enough to get waterbourne in a hurry. So hard frost is a danger to them because foxes can pop across the ice like Olympic skaters when they want to.

Now as you know, running water doesn't freeze except in really arctic conditions and there is a brook that feeds the lake at the Ambridge end and that's always the last part to freeze, so all the ducks congregate there when hard weather sets in. Nothing very clever about that. They are just looking for the last patch of water that'll freeze over - but this year for some reason or other the brook was running low and the sluggish flow combined with the bitter wind had frozen the inlet, so I expected to see the whole flock of duck take off and fly away to the river, which never freezes up. But I needn't have worried! They congregated in the centre of the lake and simply swam round and round in circles. It was a fine example of what a wonderful thing instinct is. You see they somehow knew that if they kept a patch of water moving by swimming, it wouldn't freeze, and when they'd settled on the size of patch they could keep open, they took it in turns to swim round, about half of them swimming while the others rested on the edge, and this way they kept their safe open patch of water in the middle.

I gave my company for dinner my Great Pike which was roasted...

A couple of Sundays back after service I found myself starting off for home at the very moment when Mr Adamson was starting off for his. What got us on to the subject of food was when I told him what a mighty fine sermon he'd preached and how he'd earned every mouthful of his dinner. 'Thanks, Tom,' he said. 'Glad you enjoyed it and I daresay as I'll enjoy my dinner too come to that. Though I'm glad it's not going to be the sort of meal as a certain country parson of Norfolk would have sat down to a couple of centuries ago.'

And he told me as lots of country parsons in the 18th century spent most of their time riding to hounds, fishing, going on picnics, practising archery, attending receptions with the gentry - and writing diaries. Oh, yes, they was great diary-writers these old-time country parsons and the greatest of them all, he said, was this fellow James Woodforde of Norfolk, whose

Diary of a Country Parson was a classic of its kind and if I could spare a moment to step into the vicarage he'd show me what he meant about his meals.

'How'd you fancy this for your Sunday dinner, Tom - listen - Boiled tench, pease soup, a couple of boiled chicken and pig's face, hashed calf's head, beans, roasted rump of beef - second course - roasted ducks and green peas, a very fine leveret roasted, strawberry cream, jelly, various puddings, etc., dessert...' 'Well!' said I, 'he must have had company.' The vicar said, 'Oh, yes,' he thought they'd sat down four to that little lot. 'Not quite like that with country parsons now, Tom, but I have got my favourite lunch coming up.' 'And what might that be?' says I. 'Toad-in-the-hole,' says he and went on his way.

There's something I haven't told you about and that's that we've had quite a plague of collared doves in Ambridge lately. You know them, rather pretty little birds like the turtle doves that come in summer and sing the laziest, most tuneful song in nature. Or I think they do. But collared doves stay all the year round and make the most monotonous co-coo-cooing it's been my misfortune to have to listen to. They've colonised the suburbs round big towns just as much as the country, but what took my attention the other day was how clever they are at finding new sources of food. I've been helping George put corn out for the pheasants lately and these collared doves have cottoned on. They hang around on the tree tops, and the moment one finds corn, the others see him and they all dive down together and make short work of it - and it's goodbye to our pheasants' dinner.

Do you know I reckon there have been more changes in the countryside in my lifetime than in the couple of hundred years before. I don't mean just grubbing up hedges for bigger fields, or combine harvesters instead of old-fashioned binders for harvesting corn. And I don't even mean replacing horses by tractors, but what I do mean is that there has been more change in the way we live in the countryside. And not all for the better neither to my mind.

When I started work nearly everyone lived on the job. Every

farmer had his own farm workers' cottages and when he took a man on he found him a house. Senior men, cowmen and waggoners and shepherds anyroad, and young single men, lived in. You see most old-fashioned farmhouses had huge attics going right across the roof-space. Half went on one side of the house and half the other. And the farmer and his wife slept in the middle, or their bedroom was between two staircases that went up to each of the rooms. And it was all very practical because the lads slept in one lot, and the girls in the other, so there was no chance of hanky-panky after lights out!

You see too, there were a lot more men working on a farm than there are now. Before everything got mechanised it took about a man to fifty acres, so a farm of 300 acres would have six men working on it, perhaps four of them living-in, instead of the two or three on well-run farms today.

And of course, a farm of that size would probably have a dairy maid and a couple of girls in the house but as I told you they slept on the other side of the main bedroom!

Now a good many farm workers live miles away in some village or other and commute to work in cars, the same as folk in cities do, and their old farm cottages are often used by weekenders from the towns, which doesn't please everyone in the country I can tell you.

Several nights lately I've seen the glow of fires shining here and there against the sky. Not big fires like folks makes up for Guy Fawkes night, no, the fires I'm talking about are the last burnings of brushwood from the hedge-trimming as always starts late autumn and goes on most of the winter. It's the first hedge-trimmings as makes the biggest fires but these smaller ones are the last of them. And they always looks to me as if they're really Old Winter's funeral pyre, as you might say, before we gets to spring.

And talking of spring you may not believe me but I've seen hawthorn in bud *and* leaf, way ahead of its normal time. And the blackthorn - that's the blossom of the sloes - was full out over Loxley way a fortnight back. I could hardly believe my eyes and almost thought as I must have had a glass or two of sloe gin! But there it was right enough, blossom white as snow and well before the leaf of course. It's usually around early March when the blackthorn blooms and when it does, that's what they calls 'blackthorn winter', since there's often as not a bitter wind and a sprinkle of real snow to match up with all the white flowers of the sloe-bushes.

Another thing as you sees around the roads and lanes this time of year is tractors pulling trailers piled high with spuds. They're the main crop as was lifted well afore Christmas and which has been stored between straw bales in the barns these past weeks, and now the trailers is taking them to be riddled and cleaned up and sorted out before they're ready for market. And all this kind of thing is the end of winter work before the farmers takes off their jackets to get stuck into spring - so I hope you've got your bonemeal spread and your apple trees sprayed, because it won't be long now!

March

If you can plant your foot upon nine daisies then spring has come.

Do you know how daisies got their name? Well, once they were called 'day's eye' or the 'eye of day' and I believe the old poets called them 'stars of the earth'. And talking of that, the month got its name from Mars, who was the old Romans' God of War - and I suppose this might be because with the winds and that, it's always a boisterous month is March. But of course, it's also the first month of spring and you can hear the early weaned lambs bleating, while the hedges are budding, the violets are out, and there are daffodils everywhere. And, of course, the birds are busy making their nests, though the thrushes and blackbirds are already sitting, but a lot of these early eggs will be carried off by magpies, jays and carrion crows. Another thing that's going on where there are still small ponds to be found, is that the frogs and toads will be spawning now, so before long there will be thousands of tadpoles about, because one frog can lay up to four thousand eggs - so if any more than two always survived to grow up we'd soon have a plague of frogs like they once had in Egypt!

They do say you know, that 'A peck of March dust is worth a King's ransom' because the farmers want to get on with their sowing and don't want the land wet for it, but it may surprise you that March is one of the worst months for fires in the country because all the sap is down and the bracken and grass has had the whole winter to get brittle and really dead and, of course, there's the winds to fan a fire too.

Now there's a big rookery in the woods not far from our cottage and the other day I was watching them rebuilding their nests, and a lot of them were pulling their old nests to pieces and moving them higher up - 'the higher they build the finer the summer' the old saying has it - and what a cawing and croaking and carry-on they makes of it. You never knows whether the cock-birds is singing love-songs to their mates or swearing when they've dropped a stick, or even cheering when they gets one nicely into place.

Now the shooting season's over I've been giving Gordon and George a hand catching up with the vermin. I haven't been doing any trapping myself because I haven't the time now with Mr Woolley's Garden Centre to look after, but what I have been able to do has been quite a help to them. You see all wild animals are creatures of habit. They use the same runs and the same holes, year after year. Don't ask me how they do it, because I don't know, but I'll tell you one thing - if you catch a whole litter of rats by putting a trap where they run through a hedge, next year other rats will still use the same place - but how they know about it I can't tell you.

I remember one year a stoat played lights out with my young pheasants until I caught her. And the very next week another one started to use the same place - and do even more damage - before I nabbed her too. After that I kept a trap permanently set in the same spot and that settled it.

So what I've been doing this year is take little walks round the shoot of an evening, just looking at the spots where I was always successful and if there's any signs of rats or other vermin, I've been able to pinpoint the spot Gordon should concentrate on.

I was driving over to have a word with Harry Booker in Penny Hassett the other day and when I come to a bend in the road it looked somehow different. I couldn't think what it was till I had a good look at the place on my way back. Then I realised they'd cut down the big old ash-tree as had been standing there dead for all of fifteen years, and that old ash had been such a part of the Penny Hassett road that you'd always tell strangers asking their way, 'First left after you pass an old dead ash-tree.'

Now some folk find a dead tree depressing, but somehow I don't. It's a skeleton all right, but those old dry bones of that old ash had a fine proportion about them. What's more, if the old tree had no life of its own left, there was plenty of life about it. There's been jackdaws, three pairs of them, nesting in hollows of that old tree these past ten years. One year there was nut-hatches and two years running a pair of lesser spotted woodpeckers. And almost every day, whatever the time of year, a big old carrion crow perched on the topmost branch. They loves the tops of dead trees, does carrion crows, and although I've no great love for them, they looks just right top of a dead tree somehow.

Yes, a regular old tenement you might say was that ash-tree, and I reckon as a sad old carry-on the jackdaws must have made when they were suddenly left homeless. But I reckon as the tree came down afore they'd laid their new season's eggs, and I bet you they've all moved over to the church tower in Penny Hassett by now.

Mind you, the farmer who cut the tree down won't go short of good firing for next winter.

I've just been watchin' our white blackbird. Oh, I know that sounds daft, but we really have had a white one all the winter. A proper albino he is with pink eyes. When he's in condition - and he's in perfect breeding condition now - his feathers shine whiter than snow. And we've enjoyed watchin' him because as he's so white we've been able to see for ourselves how far he goes, and how often he comes to feed, and where he roosts.

If you tell these birdwatcher chaps that you've had a blackbird for years and that he always nests in the same bush they says, 'How do you know it's the same bird? They all look the same so the one that nested in your garden last year may be miles away by now. Or eaten by the cat!' There's no answer to that, of course. You can't prove it's the same bird but we've never seen Snowy, as we call him, more than half a mile from the house. And he soon sees-off any rivals who come inside his territory.

Well, this week he's got himself a mate, and they've started to build in the holly bush down by the garden gate, so Prue and I are all steamed up waiting to see what colour the youngsters will be. I know it's counting our chickens before the eggs are laid but it will be interesting to see whether they have another albino, or if they're all dark like Mum.

And I'll tell you another thing that's interesting. When I was a kid no keeper would have waited to see what happened to a white blackbird or any other rarity. He'd have shot it and had it stuffed and put in a glass case. The Big House and the keeper's cottage always had cases and cases of stuffed white stoats and black foxes, rare birds, and pressed flowers, and butterflies pinned out in drawers. So we have progressed a bit because the only place you see such things now is at auction sales at country houses - so that's one good thing has happened.

You know old Walter Gabriel was having a lot of trouble with his roof not long ago what with the thatch going and death watch beetle and one thing and another, well there's some folks as says that thatching's a dying craft and that before long if someone wants to have his roof re-thatched there'll be nobody to take it on. That is unless he decides to go in for this new-style thatching with some kind of man-made artificial straw. Now I've got nothing against the people who've been clever enough to think it up for such folks as wants something in a hurry, and says quite proudly as 'you'd never know the difference'. Well,that's as may be, and good luck to them, I says.

But as for thatching proper being on its way out - we-ell, I have my doubts if what I saw in Little Croxley last week is anything to go by. You see, when we think about thatchers it's generally one old chap up a ladder as comes to mind. But this wasn't one old chap but three young ones, and was they going at it! Making a beautiful job of it, they was too.

Well, it being around dinner-time, I thought I'd drop into the Little Croxley pub as a change from The Bull. And sure enough about five past one in came these three young fellows, all of them in their middle twenties I'd say. Two of them was farmers' sons and the third believe it or not, was the son of a chartered accountant in Borchester, who said as he fancied a life in the fresh air rather than doing sums indoors. And one of them said his Dad grows the long straw especially for them. I never seen three happier, healthier young fellows in my life. Oh, they might earn more in a Birmingham factory but that was the life for them, they said - and it did me a power of good to hear it, I can tell you.

I was up in Martha Woodford's shop a day or two back, and what did I see? What I always calls the first real sign of spring - a rack of new packets of seed making a fine old flower-and-vegetable show at one end of the counter - though mind you, we've had ours on show at the Garden Centre for some time now. The seedsmans' catalogues as comes through the post are one thing but the packets right under your eyes are quite another though. 'Come on there,' they seem to say, 'make your choice, pay your money, take us home, and then get cracking once the time's right in the garden.'

Oh, but they're a right proper temptation seed-packets come springtime - larger than life and twice as colourful! Blue and scarlet flax, gaillardias big as windmills, cornflower, nemesia, morning glory, clarkia, nasturtium, sweet-pea, snap-dragon - you don't know which way to turn once you starts looking at them. But it's the vegetables I like to see - just look at those onions bigger'n cooking apples, marrowfat peas, four different kinds of lettuce, ah, and what about having a go at these courgette things instead of marrows for a change?

And that reminds me of a chap as I knows in the trade who has some green-houses and a patch of nursery garden over at Westbury. A couple of years back a customer comes to him for four dozen dwarf dahlias to set in some flower-beds up against the front of his cottage. 'You're too late, mate,' says the nursery garden chap, 'sold right out of dwarfs, saving that box of throw-outs over there. Weaklings they are, but you're welcome to try 'em. They won't do nothing, but help yourself.'

Do nothing! Why, come August those 'dwarfs' was all of six foot high with shaggy great pink blooms on them a foot across, and the chap as had taken them couldn't see out of his window!

Yesterday morning, I had to run over to Borchester to chase up some lengths of chain-link fencing. Naturally enough my Prue said as there were some things she wanted in the town, and if it was all the same to me she'd come along too. Well, just you try and stop a woman who doesn't find on any day of the week that there's 'some things she wants in Borchester'! 'Besides, Tom,' she says 'there's something special about Borchester of a Saturday morning. It's different from any other day of the week.'

And right enough she is too. On a Saturday morning a chap finds he wants a new hammer, or some screws, or staples, or a few feet of chicken wire. So he says to his Missus - 'Just got to rush into Borchester for half an hour, my dear.' And if he's got any sense he's on his way before she says: 'Oh, if you're going into Borchester, there's one or two things as I wants too...'

Well, when we got there my Prue goes her way and I goes mine, for I'm not one for hanging around a woman's skirts when she's shopping, and not for waiting about outside shops neither.

Of course, Saturday's got a week-end air about it - all smiles and casual clothes with nothing urgent about it like there is on a Market Day. It's the day for buying pots of paint, and new paint brushes, and rummaging around the antique shops, and looking at the week's new set of photographs as always hangs in the windows of *The Borchester Echo*.

Then what's a Saturday morning without a pint in the snug of The Red Lion? You gets all the town worthies in there from the town clerk to the top vet, and always in his corner old Sam Cardew, the leader of the Borchester bellringers. Mind you, it took me quite a while to pluck up the courage to go into that snug which you might call a kind of council of the elders. But I reckon they've accepted me now, and when it comes to news and views, I'd say as the Red Lion snug just *is* Borchester on a Saturday morning.

Takes the first warm day of spring to bring the bees out, doesn't it? I don't say as there was a great crowd of bees everywhere the other day but bees there certainly was, some of them snouting around in the violets and the first flowers of the aubretia, and dipping into the crocuses; and there was a fair number of 'em busy around the alighting boards front of the hives.

'Spring-cleaning,' says old Reuben. 'That's what they're up to. Hives gets quite a lot of rubbish lying around in 'em after the last season and the little ladies is fetching it out. Cleanest things in the world, is bees. Never foul the hive, the worker bees. If we get a couple of fine days like this in early springtime, out they'll come and what a relief it'll be to them. The 'cleansing flight' we bee chaps calls it. Oh, yes, a day like this un's right welcome to the bees and the chap as keeps 'em.'

D'you know I've been up with the lark all this week helping Gordon going after egg thieves? Not humans or rats, as you might think, but carrion crows.

You see the wild ducks, the mallard, that live on the lake at Arkwright Hall are laying now and they're not stupid! They don't choose obvious places round the side of the lake for their nests, they pick thickets of rush or bracken or rhododendron, anything up to half a mile from the water. It takes them about a fortnight to lay a clutch of eggs and they can't start to sit until the clutch is all there, because they want all the ducklings to hatch on the same day. So just as it's getting light they fly off the lake and sneak up to the nest to lay an egg every day. When they've laid it, they cover the nest with twigs or leaves, or when the clutch is nearly complete, with feathers. That's the origin of 'feathering your nest' you see! Then they sneak away and leave it hidden so it's almost impossible to find except by sheer luck.

But carrion crows, they don't rely on luck. They know ducks lay first thing in the morning, so *they* get up at crack of dawn too, and they choose a vantage point, high up in an isolated tree and sit waiting patiently for a duck to leave her nest. They mark the spot she came from and as soon as she is gone, they steal her eggs. Now no good keeper's going to stand for that, so Gordon has seen to it that there are a good few less crows about than there were!

We had some strangers in The Bull the other night and old Walter was teasing them a bit, you know, going through the old rigmarole of conning them for a drink, but it was obvious they'd heard the old saying that if you want to find a fool in the country you should take him with you. And then we started talking about the real differences between townsfolk and countryfolk. I wonder if you've ever stopped to think about it, have you?

Of course, the real thing is the size of our communities. In a village with only a few hundred people, you know everybody by sight. And they know you. So when a stranger comes everybody tries to find out what he's like. Although he don't know them, everybody knows him. Or wants to. It doesn't matter how isolated your cottage is, there's always eyes watching every visitor you have and tongues speculating about who he is and why he came. But they tell me you can live in a block of flats in a town for years - and never know your next door neighbour.

Now if you're one who's got something to hide, you wouldn't like it here in Ambridge. But of course, we don't look on it as idle curiosity so much as friendly interest. And you'd find how true that was when something goes wrong. If you get laid up with flu or something, there's always someone to do your shopping, or cooking, or help you over the stile.

And then in a village so many of us are related. We've all grown up together, so we naturally marry someone we've known since we were kids. So the first thing strangers coming into a village have to learn, is to guard their tongues if they criticise anyone. They are probably talking to his cousin!

To me, March means hares. Mad hares, that have lost their fear of man, and chase each other round in circles of love as their courtship dance skims them over the green fields with the grace of an Olympic skater. And as the rhythm hots up, tempers fray, and there's more brawling and skirmishing than you'd ever see in polite society anywhere. It isn't the come-out-in-the-yard-and-fight-me-for-her sort either. Most of the scuffles are not between rival bucks about who shall have first choice. They're between bucks and does, and when one buck gets a bit over-eager and pushes his luck too far, the darling of his heart stands up on her hind legs and boxes his ears for him. And he's not as chivalrous as he might be either, so he stands up and punches her back - but he isn't in real earnest, so he gives way first, and thinking she really *is* the winner, she chases him round a couple more circuits of their ritual dance. Then off they go again but the tempo gradually changes and the doe doesn't play quite so hard-to-get, so when she does box his ears, it's more of a love-tap than a blow in defence of her honour.

Any month will send hares mad if the weather and conditions are right, but March is the month when they really go mad and throw all caution to the winds.

There was a chap I once knew who came from Essex way and he told me he'd seen a couple of big Jack hares standing on their hind legs one night boxing like they were Mohammed Ali and Joe Frazier, really going at each other punch for punch. And there wasn't just one doe sitting and looking on as there usually is. But this time, there were ten or more and they was sitting round in a perfect circle. Of course, some of them could have been Jacks waiting their turn to have a go at the winner, but anyroad, it looked like a properly organised affair according to him. And he watched it for all of two minutes. Then suddenly it was all over with no clear winner as far as he could see, and both the boxers dropped on to their four feet and ran off in opposite directions through the ring of spectators - and then they scattered all over the place too. And when he went into his local and told them about it, they said he should take more water with it - but he always swore he saw it.

There's all sorts of superstitions about hares - some says they brings on melancholy in anyone as eats them; and other folks believes they changes sex every year; and there's others who says it's bad luck if a hare crosses your path, for witches can turn themselves into hares as easy as winking - but that's all a lot of nonsense, of course.

I was going for an early stroll before breakfast the other day when I thought I saw a fox come out of the wood and disappear into a dense bramble. 'Nothing remarkable about that' you might say but you see that 'fox' didn't have a proper brush. He looked like a bobtailed 'un, with only a stump about four inches long. Not only that, he'd got it stuck up in the air and the bit sticking up looked white. Almost as if whatever had broken his tail off had skinned it and left it without any fur.

Now I only got a glimpse of him but my instinct told me to be wary because there was something else odd about him. He didn't slink along, cunning-like, as foxes usually do. And something about his movement reminded me of a hedgehog - although of course, he was much bigger than a hedgehog.

Well I was so puzzled that I sneaked up to the bramble brake where he'd disappeared and got between the cover and the wood and stood as still as a statue to see what happened. After about twenty minutes I heard a faint rustle and a little brown animal popped out of the far side of the brambles. It certainly wasn't a fox, although it was about the same size and coloured reddish, but when it got into the open, I could see that it was a very small deer, and then of course, I knew what it was. It was the very first muntjak to come into our area.

Now muntjak are the smallest deer you can find in this country. The Duke of Bedford brought the first ones from China in the last century and some escaped from his park at Woburn. Barking deer, they call them, because they are much noisier than our native ones. And they've been spreading northwards ever since, and they've colonised about as far as Warwickshire now but they're so secretive and live in such thick cover that it's hard to see them. So I'm keeping quiet about ours in the hopes that he has brought a mate with him so we can have some more.

Do you know on St Patrick's day, the 17th, I heard the first chiff-chaff of the year? Yes, there the little fellow was in a thicket back of our cottage making himself known with that call as he gets his name from - 'chiff-chaff - chiff-chaff - chiff-chaff', just a day or two ahead of the official first day of spring. Of course the great tit starts up with his 'teacher-teacher' business round about the same time, but as he lives here all the year round he doesn't 'come with the spring on his wings' as the little chiff-chaff does, all the way from warmer climates. And it's one of the best signs that the winter is behind us, and that after all, March may go out like a lamb.

April

When proud-pied April in all his trim
Hath put a spirit of youth in everything.

And that's true you know, because April is the fastest growing month in all the year - and the word itself comes from a Latin one meaning 'I open' and my word, the buds do, don't they? Of course one of the reasons is that the days are longer than the nights again and that's what makes it good for growing. And then all the fruit trees blossom - peach, cherry, plum, almond and last of all the apple, but night frosts can do a lot of damage. They used to say 'There be no warm weather till the corn-crakes croak' and corn-crakes used to be quite common when I was a lad, but the new methods of hay-harvesting have made it a much rarer bird now. In the old days when grass was cut by scythe the young birds had time to escape and because scything didn't cut so close as the mowing-machines do, the eggs often escaped too, so that explains it, doesn't it?

Well now, swallows and house-martins usually come back to us about the middle of the month, and swifts, which are often called Jack Squealer, towards the end of it. Townsfolk find it difficult to tell one from t'other but swallows have a streamer each side of their tails, and house-martins have forked tails which look 'webbed', while swifts are smoky-coloured and larger than the others and they almost never land on the ground, because their wings are so long they can hardly get airborne again unless someone picks them up and launches them. But this year, it was one day last week actually, I heard my Prue suddenly call out from the garden. 'Tom,' she shouts, '*Tom* come out here quick.' She sounded in such a fluster I thought there must be at least a cow got into the garden. So I rushes out, and there's no cow of course, only my Prue standing staring out over the meadow, pointing now this way and now that. 'They're back,' she shouts, 'Tom, they're back - look...' And sure enough they were back - leastways one of them was - flying low over the meadow, backwards and forwards, and looking very tired on the wing - the first 'swallow' of the year come home all the way from Africa - and what's more it was ours! We just stood there, the pair of us, excited as a couple of kids, watching that little bird. 'Three days late this year,' says Prue. 'They usually turns up around the thirteenth or fourteenth. I daresay we'll see his mate tomorrow.'

Well, if this was one of ours, there'll be no shutting the doors of the shed where I keeps my truck for the next few months, for that's where they nests every year on top of the centre crossbeam. And a proper old mess they makes of my truck too, especially after the first brood arrives and sits there like a row of little clergymen. But I don't mind, I feel it's an honour to have them picking out your home to share.

Folks often wonder why the swifts, and the swallows, and the martins, flies all those thousands of miles to spend the summer with us. Well, Robin Freeman explained it to me once - it's on account of the long daylight, which means enough insects for feeding the family. The little ones eats heaven knows how many times their own weight when they're in the nest, and in the tropics with the shorter days, the youngsters would starve, no matter how hard the parents worked. It's an extraordinary thing nature, isn't it?

Did you know that if you see two crows, they're rooks, and if you see one rook, it's a crow! Or so we say in the country. And it's not as daft as you might think. You see, crows are pretty solitary birds, and you don't often get more than one or two together, except when they flock-up in winter roosts. But rooks are as gregarious as ladies at a coffee morning, so you don't often see a rook on her own, she always likes plenty of other rooks to go yakitty-yak with. And my word, don't they do a lot of damage, crows, not only to game but to song birds too!

And at this time of year, of course, rooks are nesting. Now, although I've spent a lifetime as a keeper, I do love a rookery. They build great clusters of nests, sometimes several hundred strong, high up in the trees before the leaves are out. Don't ask me how they choose their building sites because I don't know but once they pick a site they take a lot of shifting. And they don't seem to mind disturbance and noise, so you often see rookeries in towns. For instance, there's one right in the shopping area in the middle of Cheltenham, and the cawing of the rooks makes a nice change from the roar of traffic, I can tell you.

You may be surprised when I say I've had a wild duck's nest in the garden this year, right in sight of the kitchen window where I could keep my eye on it. And only an ex-keeper like me knows how important that is, because before the leaves are really out, duck eggs are very conspicuous so most of the first clutches get eaten by crows, or magpies, or jays. In fact you might say that wild ducks are so prolific that the eggs they lay are more of a crop to feed predators than a means of supplying replacement wild ducks!

But do you know where ducks usually lay? Not in the reeds along the edges of pools, as you might expect, there are too many enemies there who want duckling for dinner. Or duck egg for breakfast! And they're not very neighbourly either, because it is not by any means unknown for one duck, or more likely a drake, to drown another one's ducklings. They don't believe in encouraging competition for what food there is, you see! So you'll very often find a wild duck's nest quite a long way from water. Half a mile or so, anyway. She chooses a really well hidden place to hide her eggs and she doesn't take her youngsters down to the water till they're strong enough to hide in the reeds for safety. Now you'd probably expect such clumsy, flat-footed creatures that don't perch, to pick a site in a thick clump of nettles, or bramble, or rhododendron, to hide the nest - and you'd often be right. But the nest in our garden this year would have surprised you. It was up a tree! And it seemed odd to me to find a web-footed bird nesting up a tree.

Our tree's a pollarded willow, and she'd made her nest in the hollow in the crown, and when the ducklings hatched they launched themselves into space and floated down to earth as light as thisledown with never an injury to any of them - so they'll all grow up safe and sound to have little ducklings of their own in time.

I wonder what spring means to you? Now be careful with your answer because it may give your character away! If you say snowdrops, and primroses, and bird-song, I might think you're a bit of a visionary. A romantic. Or if you say blackthorn blossom I shall think of sloe-gin at Christmas, and that you might be the practical type. But in the country spring is hard work. Imagine starting to plough a hundred acre field at dawn one morning. That's work. Cold noisy work reeking of diesel fumes. But it's satisfying, creative work. And this spring - well I've never seen so much ground so well worked and drilled - with reasonable weather there should be a good harvest - but you never know, do you?

There's no sight in the world spells spring more clearly to me than half a dozen lambs chivvying, and bouncing, and butting each other for the prize of standing for a few seconds on top of a fallen log or hummock of soil - their 'castle' - before a rival tips them off.

Now in hill country, flocks were always brought down to the homesteads when the weather got bad in winter. If they'd been left to lamb in the open they'd have lost a good few lambs to foxes and quite a lot to the weather.

On our sort of farms at Ambridge we have them into the farmyards to lamb, where we can keep an eye on them - and that's another spring job. A spring chore you might call it, because ewes are often awkward mums and being midwife to them is hard and messy work - and often a very cold one too. If that's what spring means to you, spring is pretty uncomfortable, I can tell you! Wise farmers like Dan time their lamb crop so they're ready to go out in the fields just when the first tender bite of spring grass is sprouting. And that's easy enough, if you don't put the ram in with your flock until five months before you want the first lamb.

Last night in The Bull, we was talking about fish for Good Friday. When I was a kid we always had pancakes on Shrove Tuesday, and fish on Good Friday. Of course there's a lot of folk who always has fish every Friday, but what we was on about last night was how they always managed to get it in the old days before they had steam trawlers, and deep freezers, and that sort of thing. And it was old Walter Gabriel who come up with the answer. One answer anyhow. He said as the monks had what they called fish-stews, which were pools like chicken runs, where they could keep the fish they caught alive till they wanted 'em for the table.

And that reminded me of a picture that hung over the fireplace when I was a kid. There was a row of monks dressed in their long cassocks and hoods sitting by a lake with rods stuck out waiting for a bite. And the caption underneath said 'Tomorrow will be Friday - and we've caught no fish today!' They weren't really as casual about it as that though. The chaps who built monasteries and stately homes had a marvellous eye for country. They always chose places with wonderful views, where nature provided all mod. cons. Wood for fires, game for the larder, good land for farming, and above all an endless supply of fresh water. I've never heard of a monastery without its spring and its pools. And if there weren't pools, they flooded the valleys and filled them from the streams. Then they stocked them with fish, so Friday dinner wasn't such a chancy business as you might think. But modern scientists are going one better like they often do. They've discovered that some fish grow faster if the water is kept a little bit warmer than usual. Now, it so happens that electric power stations which use water for cooling, discharge warm water into the rivers close by. Conservationists calls it hot water pollution but it looks like it may be warm water enrichment now that it may be making the fish grow faster!

The church bells will be ringing all over the country on Good

Friday and the Sunday, and there'll be that happy Easter feeling inside us whether we're practising Christians or not. I'm not one for sermonising as you might say, but I really do believe as there's something about Easter that we can't put words to, quite apart from it being a nice spring holiday. Take Good Friday, for example. That's a strange sort of a day, particularly in country villages like Ambridge. It's a Sunday as doesn't feel like a proper Sunday, with farm work stopping at noontide just as the doors of The Bull open as though it was a Sunday. Oh, the pints goes round right enough, but I never feel as the Good Friday pint's quite the same as a Sunday morning one.

But there's one thing as is certain about Good Friday in the country. Provided it's not belting down with rain, this is the day when everyone gets busy in the garden or the allotment, getting the spades and the forks into the ground, turning that old slag heap of winter into a fine tilth, drawing out the drills and getting the seeds in. Oh! but the smell of the soil turned over in the spring - there's nothing sweeter in the whole year to my mind.

And provided the weather's right, the village really seems to come alive this week-end with the walkers, and the cyclists, and folks in cars having picnics on Ambridge Green. There's some as grumbles that such folks spoils the village of a Bank Holiday weekend, but I'm not one of them. Provided they behaves themselves - well, who are we that's lucky enough to live in the country to blame others for enjoying it like we do?

What with it staying light late, and the school holidays, Ambridge seems swarming with kids wherever you go now, and last night down by Arkwright Hall lake I watched some of them for nearly an hour, because I thought as they was up to some mischief - and I couldn't quite make out what. They kept very still these kids for a long time, and then I noticed some of them had field glasses and it dawned on me what they was. They were young bird watchers. *And* they'd been to the estate office and got permission before they'd come! So I went up to them to see what they were doing and if I could help. They'd been all round checking on a recent census of birds' nests, and while they were at it, they were looking for duck nests, and moorhens, and small birds.

And that reminded me of my young days, I can tell you. Birds-nesting was all the rage then, not just to look and make notes as these youngsters were doing, but to steal the eggs. Mind you, we weren't the villains you might think. We had a very strict code and never took more than one egg from a nest and wild horses wouldn't have dragged out of us where the nests were. And I think it was my collection of birds eggs which first got me keen on natural history, so I hope on balance, I've done more good than harm! But these kids down by the lake, knew every bird by sight, and every song by sound. And what I liked about them was that they went about so quietly. No noise or disturbance, so I'm sure they saw more of the birds than the birds saw of them!

But instead of finding nests like I used to do, I make the nests come to me now. You see, gamekeepers encourage brambles, and rushes, and shrubs for their pheasants to nest in and I use the same principle for garden birds - so could you if you wanted to, and you'd probably get as much fun out of it as I do, even if your garden's no bigger than a pocket handkerchief. This is what you do - you leave a bushy bit of privet hedge, or a holly thicket unclipped. It mayn't look very tidy but I bet you'll soon have a nest of hedge-sparrows in it. Mind you, they're not sparrows at all really, but dunnocks, and wonderful for killing garden pests they are. And I've put several nest boxes up, all on the shady side of trees, and out of reach of cats - and two pair of blue tits are sitting on eggs already, and a robin has started negotiations for a kettle in the corner and I reckon that lot'll kill more garden pests than a bucket of pesticides will!

Spending so long rearing pheasants has given me a sort of eye for what birds consider 'desirable building plots', so I spend a few hours every spring scheming where to put what box, or which bush to leave untrimmed - and then I sit back to see if I've made a good forecast!

Mind you sometimes, I didn't forecast right at all. Last year when Prue's peas came up and I wanted to put the pea-sticks further up, I couldn't. An old blackbird had chosen my row of sticks to build her nest in so, of course, I couldn't disturb her.

The peas seemed to do just as well so it didn't matter after all!

I've been thinking about the economics of game-keepering lately. Even when I was a lad, shooting was a rich man's sport. In those days it cost about seven and six to rear a bird and put it in the wood, and that was quite a bit of money then. A cartridge cost six pence and the game dealer only wanted to pay about half a crown each for the birds, so they used to say 'up goes seven and six, bang goes a tanner, and down comes half a crown.' And it's worse now. Last season the price we got for pheasants averaged about seventy pence, and they cost anything up to a fiver each to rear. That included the keeper's wages, the rent of the shoot, food, rearing pens - the lot. Including a van or landrover for the keeper! When I started we had Shank's Pony, or we rode a bike. That was a wonderful, silent way of stealing down country lanes, peeping over the hedges and surprising intruders. But too much like hard work for 'em today! So like it or not, I reckon we shall either have to cut the costs of shooting - or there will be less and less folk who can afford to pay chaps like me, however much they want to.

But I often wonders if visitors to the countryside realise just how much our generation owes to the sporting men of the last century. In those days whole estates were laid out to make hunting and shooting more successful. They planted little spinneys and copses about in parkland, specially sited so they would attract and 'hold' birds which could be driven over the guns to the next spinney or cover. It's that wonderful patchwork of parkland and open fields, dotted with little woods and trees, which make English scenery so much better than anywhere else in the world.

Now, if I go into a strange part of the country I love to climb the nearest hill and look at the layout of the land. I can nearly always see, not only how beautiful it is, but exactly why each group of trees and cover was planted. And I like to think that these pleasant views were often the result of team-work between old-fashioned keepers and their bosses, even if sport, not scenery, was in their minds when they planned it all out!

There's been a lot in the papers lately about the conservationists' campaign to Save the Wetlands. They're busy saving places ranging from marshes and lakes to village ponds, in fact anywhere where wildlife might be threatened - and a very good thing too! And I daresay you'll remember how busy Laura was getting people to help clear out our Ambridge village pond a while back.

Of course, there were often little ponds in the corner of fields which were useful for watering stock put out to graze. And you can imagine that a herd of cattle which are not exactly house-trained, didn't exactly purify the water when they cooled off in summer heat by standing in it. So when it became possible to plough-in long lengths of plastic pipe instead of digging trenches for expensive copper pipe, a lot of farmers provided troughs in their fields and mains water for their cattle and the ponds weren't needed any more. Mind you, I don't think there was as much risk from stock drinkin' out of little natural pools as some make out. There was a lot of superstition about it. Newts, for instance!

When I was a kid, we called newts 'wet-efts' or 'askers', and really believed they could spit fire! They don't, of course, and in fact they do a lot of good by eating mosquito larvae. At this time of the year newts congregate in the sort of little pools as the conservationists are trying to save. They go there to breed, which they do by laying eggs in strings of spawn instead of masses, like frog-spawn.

Farming folk had another superstition about newts which isn't quite so obvious. They thought that if a cow, or especially a horse, drank from a pond where newts were swimming and swallowed one by accident, it would get most terrible colic. But I reckon if the animal did get a bit of bellyache, it would be from eating too much young clover, which is just at its most tender when the newts are breeding!

Now talking of pools and ponds, there's something that happens at about this time of year or a bit earlier, I'd like to tell you about. All last winter they've been lying murky and muddy and scummy - then suddenly - they clears! There's blobs of brown, fluffy bubbles come to the surfaces from down below as if the pond was giving itself a spring-clean. Then as they disappears, there's the whole pond under your eyes so clear you can see right down to the bottom. You can see the little minnows and stickle-backs flashing for shelter in the reeds, and if there's bigger fish you'll like as not see them trying to get away from you. Then, of course, there's the frog-spawn in the corners and the toad-spawn in strings of jelly slung around the water-plants. And what kid can resist taking frog-spawn home and waiting for the babies to hatch out in jam-jars. Though sometimes I wish as they wouldn't, cos there's fewer frogs about than there used to be. But there, it's 'tiddler-time' for village kids everywhere, and I like to see them with their little nets and jam-jars, looking so intense about it all. They're learning something about nature, and kids 'tiddlering' have been part of Ambridge ever since I was one of them myself.

Sweet April showers
Do spring May flowers.

But they spring April ones too! There are the wood anemones, they're sometimes called 'granny's nightcap' and sometimes 'wind-flowers', they cover the woodlands with white sheets of flowers before the trees come into leaf, and there's blue-bells, and wild daffodils, of course, and dandelions (I'm sure you tried to tell the time when you were a kid by blowing the dandelion clocks and counting how many blows it took to get all the feathery white seed heads off) and I bet you didn't know there are more than a hundred different species of dandelion in the British Isles, did you?

Towards the end of the month cowslips appear - the separate flowers or petals are sometimes known as 'peeps', and old Martha will be picking them out to make her cowslip wine before long, and very good it is too!

Prue's first peas will be showing soon, the spinach will be rampant, our rhubarb will be looking like a tropical plant, and we always try to have a dish of new potatoes on Good Friday - grown under glass, of course. Oh yes, and talking of Good Friday you did know you should plant your parsley then, didn't you? And that you should never transplant it, or a death or bad luck will come? Oh, and one more thing - in the old days there used to be a country saying that seeds should be planted under a waxing moon, and never under an waning one, so do be careful, won't you?

May

If you were April's lady
And I were Lord in May

I don't suppose you'd believe me if I was to tell you that I was once the May King of Ambridge, and I'm not telling you how many years ago *that* was, when I sat one down from the May Queen with a painted paper crown on my head and a willow sceptre in my hand. Not that anybody thought a lot to the May King - he was like the drone in the bee-hive while set along of the Queen bee!

I dare say they still has the Maypole and the Crowning of the May Queen in some places, but I reckon that when they do it's more self-conscious than it used to be in the old days. To us kids it was the most natural thing in the world that every first of May we started the day off before school by 'May singing' all around the village. Of course we'd learned the songs from the school teacher and practised the dancing round the maypole to an old gramophone in the playground - though on the day, it was the village cobbler what called the tune for us on his old brown fiddle.

Round about half-past seven we started off, all us boys in our Sunday best with starched collars and the girls in their pinafores led by the new May Queen and her attendants. We was all slung about with cowslips, buttercups and daisies, and we carried posies of wild flowers as we piped up *Nymphs and Shepherds, The Merry Month of May, We'll go a-Maying* and suchlike, and the pennies we collected were supposed to go to the school outing, but I can tell you as some of them found their way into the sweet shop afore we went to school.

Little Nancy Perrin was the May Queen of the year I best remembers - there was a bit of the gipsy about dark-haired Nancy and - well, I'd have given my last gob-stopper for one smile from those brown eyes! And when the Queen of the year before, crowned her with a chaplet of cowslips, I don't mind saying as my heart slipped a bit, kid though I was! Proper old sentimentalist I'm being today, so I must stop day-dreaming and get back to something else.

When I was a kid we always went rook shooting on the 10 May. Not because we thought of it as much of a sporting occasion but simply because rooks really did do farmers a lot of damage by pulling up the corn by the roots and the middle of May, just as they were leaving the nest, was the time you could thin them out most easily.

Well, things have changed since my day - and May rook shooting is a thing of the past in most places and I'm glad of it. But I'm not glad about why. Folk didn't stop shooting young rooks for sentimental reasons, you know. There are simply less rooks about than there used to be, so the damage they do makes them less of an enemy. Mind you, I never thought they did that much damage anyway. It's true they pulled out a lot of young corn but I always thought the corn they picked on had wireworm at the roots and that it was the wireworm they was after. Certainly the rooks there are about now seem to do more good than harm because the insect pests they eat more than pays for what crops they damage. And the modern farming fashion is not to shoot them but to put bird scarers in the fields, which give off a loud bang every 30 seconds or so just while the crops are extra vulnerable.

When you think about the hazards rooks've had, it's marvellous there are any about at all. Elms are one of their favourite trees to breed in and in many parts of the country, as you know, three out of every four elms have been wiped out by this terrible Dutch elm disease. Now there's an old country saying that 'rooks desert a dying tree' but like a lot of other old wives' tales, it isn't true! I know several places where they are still nesting in elms that have been dead a couple of years and if we'd had a good blow then it would have killed more young birds as they fell down with the rotten wood, than all the rook shooting parties in the country. But what really wiped the rooks out in their thousands was the poisonous pesticides farmers were using one time.

When I was a kid the young rooks were eaten in pies - a little rook and a lot of stewing steak was best - but only the breasts, thighs and wings were used because the backs, like starlings', were bitter, which is probably why cats don't like them!

And talking of rooks I wonder if you know that old country rhyme about magpies?

One, sorrow
Two, mirth
Three, a wedding
Four, birth.

And another thing, did you know it's lucky if martins build their nests against your house because they never build against one where there is strife. Did you know that?

And there's another country saying, 'A swarm of bees in May is worth a load of hay'. With the present price of sugar a swarm should be worth a pot of gold now I reckon. When bees swarm they belong to the owner only as long as he can see and follow them: but even then he can't go onto another man's land to get 'em back without permission. And if the owner of the land can catch them they are his and the original owner shouldn't really have much cause for complaint because it is considered bad bee-keeping to let them swarm because they have to waste time building up a new colony when they ought to be busy making honey. Of course it's removing the surplus queens that prevents swarming. And talking of bees has set me thinking about royal jelly, and wonderful stuff that is too. Because you see, the worker bees do all the drudgery by collecting the nectar and pollen from flowers but they can't breed because they are sexless, so all the eggs that hatch into workers have to be laid by queen bees and when the population in the hive needs renewing a queen is 'arranged' simply by feeding her a special food called royal jelly. This is reserved exclusively for queens and it produces a bee several times as big as an ordinary worker which can lay eggs for the whole of a very long life.

In the old days, nobody knew what this royal jelly really was but they did know that it was as potent as a magic wand and they naturally thought that if it could produce a fertile queen bee from what otherwise would have developed into an ordinary worker there might be no limit to what it could do to human beings. So bee keepers started collecting the royal jelly from their hives instead of leaving it for future queens. They didn't get much, of course, because queen cells are only made large enough to fit one queen bee but they reckoned that even quite a small dose might rejuvenate people because queen bees lived much longer than ordinary ones and were so fertile they laid thousands and thousands of eggs in a single lifetime. In fact they thought it might work wonders with their love life too!

As you know, the best doctors don't always pooh-pooh folklore because there is often something in it, so the medical profession has done a lot of research on the properties of this royal jelly. But if it has any of the properties that were once claimed for it, the results seem to have been more from faith than fact.

You may be surprised but although I've retired from regular game-keepering and am working in Jack Woolley's Garden Centre at Grey Gables, I still go bird-nesting night and morning because, you see, it's in my blood and I can't stop my eyes prying into every nook and corner at this time of the year. Not that I ever do the birds any harm mind, or take any eggs, it just gives me a kick to be able to find them. And I still keep up some of the other habits I developed over a lifetime as a game keeper. Only yesterday I found a robin's nest in the mossy bank by the stile in the woods near our cottage. It was low down, where dogs might smell it or cats hear the nestlings as soon as they hatch, so I took a tin of old tractor oil and spilt a drop close by. You see the stench should mask the smell from dogs, so they won't find it, and cats will be so prissy about getting their feet sticky that I hope they'll be too busy avoiding the oil to bother about the baby birds in the nest!

Now if you'd been out with me early this mornin', I'd have shown you a thrush sitting on her second clutch, a tree creeper that's just laid, wagtails feeding - and that robin I told you about before. And of course May is a wonderful month for bird-song.

Mind you I loves every season as it comes round - but I think perhaps I love May best of all. Apart from the fun of finding birds' nests and listening to their songs, I love the *greens* of May. They're so fresh and come in more shades than there are colours in the rainbow.

Grass and young corn grows faster from now to the middle of June than at any other time - and farmers who have piled so much extra nitrogen in for growth, show up their land 'greener than green', as clear as if they'd gone round with a paint brush - especially when it's dry. Because you see, a good dosing of fertiliser helps crops stand up to dry times. That's one reason why you'll see grass always looking so lush where there's been a dung patch, no matter how dried up the rest of it looks. And I suppose it was because of all the lush grass that the old Anglo-Saxons milked their cows three times a day about now and called the month Thrimilcs, though our name comes from the Latin, Maia, the Goddess of growth and increase. And, of course, the village cricket greens looks their best too at the start of the season - and very nice they do look with youngsters practising in white flannels and the old stagers coaching them.

I was watchin' some of the local kids buying sweets and ices round at Martha's shop the other day and it made me think just how lucky modern kids are compared to my day. They can spend more pocket money in a week then we had in a year.

Thinkin' it over though, I'm not so sure that we weren't luckier than them after all. You see, we had to scrat around for our cash before we could spend it because our Dads couldn't afford to give much away. And country kids had marvellous chances of making a bit for themselves then. Not just running errands and dull stuff like that I don't mean, but I was quite an expert stock keeper by the time I was eight. I swapped a pair of tame mice with a lad at school for a hazel stock to carve a walking stick out of. You see you could sell good sticks for a bob or two at the local point-to-point races then, so I developed an uncommon sharp eye for a good stick. I remembered wherever I saw a good one, waited for it to grow the right size, and cut it out in winter when the sap was down. Of course, I got caught out sometimes, because another kid might cut it first just when I'd waited a couple of years for it to grow to the right size, so I had to use my judgment whether to leave it or whether a stick in the shed was worth a bundle someone else might nab!

Well, this particular one I cut made a very nice thumb-stick, so I had no difficulty swapping it for a pair of mice. I kept them as stock mice and bred from them, and I fitted some boards along the inside wall of the fowl pen as a sort of skirting board and my young white mice took to this like tits to a nest box. They set up home behind the board - and bred like a swarm of flies. Best of all, I didn't even have to feed them because they came out at night and took the corn and scraps the fowl had left! Talk about dog-and-stick farming, I was the grand-daddy of them all! When holidays came round, all I had to do was catch up the surplus mice, take 'em into Borchester and flog 'em to the pet shop - and I was set up with pocket-money for the rest of the holidays.

All country kids used to get up to capers like that. Breeding rabbits and selling them or ferreting and selling the wild ones we caught. Or picking watercress or mushrooms or blackberries and making a copper or so out of that. There's great satisfaction in using your initiative you know.

Now I was watching Gordon Armstrong getting ready to move a batch of young pheasants yesterday - and he properly took my eye. It's all right grumbling about young gamekeepers idling around in a truck when they ought to be on Shanks's Pony, but I found another side to him. And I was surprised, for do you know he's as as good a craftesman with a scythe as chaps in my generation were. He wanted some strips of herbage short for the young birds to sun 'emselves and keep dry, and some strips long where they could find insects for food or hide if there was danger. Well, mowing machines or tractors are all right for cutting fields of hay - but they're no good for pickin' and choosin' bits and dabs, like Gordon wanted, so he was mowin' 'em by hand.

Now you can always tell a good chap with a scythe, not so much by what the job looks like as how it sounds. A sharp scythe sizzles through the grass. It hisses and whispers because the blade's so keen the stems don't even slow it as it swings. The next secret, of course, is that a man don't fit his scythe, he adjusts it to fit him. You see, the toe and heel of a scythe can be adjusted till the blade swings level, parallel to the ground, to suit the mower's natural swing and then the handle seems to have grown onto the ends of his arms. The whetstone whistles along the blade till a cut-throat razor's as blunt as a penknife by comparison - and then look out! Young Gordon was shufflin' along, gently slicing a swath as each foot stepped forward, and watchin' him I felt quite proud he used to work for me.

Those mechanical gadgets they have on farms are all very well but somehow there isn't the satisfaction in pressing a knob or a lever and having a job done for you as there is in doing it yourself with the same simple tools your ancestors used. And I've done the job often enough myself when I was young, so I know what I'm talking about.

If the apple-tree bloom in May
You can eat apple-dumplings every day.

Do you know I've never seen a year like this for blossom and wild flowers? It started off a blackthorn winter with acres of snowy white sloe blossom in the hedgerows before the leaves came out - and then there were the catkins. Right monsters, they were, fit for any flower show. Even the birch catkins seemed as long as the lambs' tails we used to call them as kids. And those that grow on pussy willows were as round and as buxom and as golden as girls on a sandy beach by the sea.

Down our lane the cow-parsley, or Queen Anne's Lace as we

call it in the country, filled the verge with a white veil that lasted longer this year than usual because the council's economy drive has stopped 'em mowing the verges. So perhaps the slump's had some benefits after all! And if you drove out into the country about a fortnight ago, there were fields so full of golden dandelions you couldn't have put an old-fashioned sixpence down between them. They were marvellous to look at but the farmers aren't so pleased about them because of course, to them they're weeds. It all depends on your point of view, don't it? As someone once said, a weed is just a wild-flower in the wrong place!

What I finds interesting is that conservationists have been saying for years that modern farming methods have almost exterminated our wild flowers. And there's no doubt chemical sprays and pesticides have altered the countryside, wiping out a lot of wild flowers that were harmless, as well as weeds that interfered with growing crops. But the freak weather, like the mild winters we've had and the drought, are making their mark too. Nature isn't that easy to beat, you know. As soon as you take the pressure off, things that you thought had gone for good come back and I'm waiting to see if some of our rare butterflies can increase again now their food plants have rallied. And if the harvest of wild fruit this autumn is as plentiful as the blossom in spring then our village shop will do a good trade in home-made wines and jams this backend and old Martha'll be kept on the go.

A voice as thrilling ne'er was heard
In spring-time from the cuckoo-bird...

One day around about dusk earlier in the month, my Prue and I heard the nightingale singing in the little coppice which lies at the back of our cottage. Now the first cuckoo in spring always sets folk talking, even before he's come. 'You heard the cuckoo yet?' folks says round about the end of March. 'Someone told me as they heard him over Darrington way yesterday morning.' And if anyone says that, you can be sure as it's a newcomer to the district because everyone in Darrington knows about that early cuckoo of theirs - because there's a young

Darrington boy as does that first cuckoo a treat and for a couple of years he fooled even the folks there themselves.

Of course the cuckoo's one thing, but the nightingale - well he's a bird of a different feather. What's more, there's not as many of them about as there used to be - but here he was that night right on our back-doorstep as you might say. Of course we was thrilled, and when he was 'jug-jugging' away out there for the next three nights we reckoned as he was there to stay. Well, at the beginning we'd just stand there in the garden listening to his song in the twilight. And what with the smell of the cow-parsley, and the moon just rising back of the trees - 'Well,' I said to myself, 'where else in the world could you find anything to touch this?'

Yet do you know that after a week I could almost have wrung that blessed bird's neck. I'd lie there in bed listening to him, then he'd stop for a while, and I'd wait for him to start up again. And when he did I'd say to myself: 'Yes, you sings beautiful, but I wish you'd shut up so's I could get a wink of sleep.' Because that's something about the nightingale singing - you feel as you've got to listen because if you don't you're missing one of the rarest sounds as was ever put on this earth. Though I don't mind admitting as it can get on your nerves after a while as I've just been telling you.

June

When June is come, then all the day
I'll sit with my love in the scented hay,
And watch the sunshot palaces high,
That the white clouds build in the breezy sky.

June is the great month for sitting in the grass and I bet you don't know how many different kinds there are, do you? Have you heard of meadow fescue, tall fescue, timothy grass, cocks foot, perennial rye-grass, black grass, common couch, tor grass, common quaking or tottering grass, false-brome, wood millet, tufted hair grass, common reed grass, needle-leaved fescue - in fact I could go on and on and on about them because the grasses are the largest and most important family of flowering plants in our islands. It's made up of the cereals, wheat, barley and oats, the grasses grown from hay, silage and grazing, and more than 150 wild species as well, so I reckon you couldn't be blamed if you couldn't put names to them all. What do you think?

But it's a wonderful month June (named after the Roman Goddess Juno, by the way) a wonderful month - trees are at their best and so are the roses. There are bees, dragonflies and butterflies about, the first peas and lettuces are with us - you want to protect your strawberries against birds and slugs by the way, and birds are after the cherries too. The red and black currants have begun to colour, the raspberries and loganberries are forming and the young birds in the nests are demanding attention - and worms. Oh, a proper busy time of the year it is, I can tell you - and I haven't mentioned the garden flowers there are about. You should just see Doris's garden at Glebe Cottage, though she can't manage as well now as she used to because of her arthritis, but it's always been a picture that garden.

In spite of its name you'll be surprised to hear June is the month for mayflies! There are about fifty kinds of them, but the two commonest are the favourites with fishermen. The fresh-water fishing season starts on 16 June of course and some people say there are more coarse fishermen in England than there are football fans!

However, I was telling you about mayflies, wasn't I? Well, they take two years to mature from the egg - and only about two days to die. When they emerge as perfect insects, they mate and the females then always fly upstream, because otherwise, you see, each season the eggs would appear further and further downstream until they finished up in the sea and then there wouldn't be any more mayflies, would there? Well the flies in each area hatch at about the same time each day, say at lunchtime or teatime and as each hatch doesn't last long the fishermen have to hang about for the next hatch so they can be sure of a good 'rise' of fish for themselves.

Delicate looking things mayflies are, with gossamer wings, but there is a darker form which the fishermen call green drakes, not because of their colour but because the artificial flies that are made to imitate them are made from the green hackle feathers of a mallard drake.

The hawthorn blossom (May blossom) dies away in June, and is followed by the creamy foam of elderflowers which make wonderful wine - you should try Martha Woodford's if you can - and the flowers are good as fritters too. You dip the whole bloom into very thick batter and fry it in very hot fat, then eat it with spinach or sugar, according to whether you want a savory or a sweet - beautiful it can be.

Did you know country kids often burn the soft pith out of

elder twigs with red hot skewers to make pea shooters? And when the twigs are used in birdcages as perches, the red mites, which bite canaries, crawl up in daytime and so you can destroy them.

I was going down the main road out of the village the other evening when I noticed two characters skulking about in a lay-by. Very suspicious they looked too. Both dressed in blue jeans with sloppy pullovers. Thick enough to keep a blizzard out. One had a fuzzy beard and they seemed to be messin' about with old empty milk bottles. So I sidled up to take a closer look at what they was doing, but instead of solving the mystery they got me more and more foxed. For as far as I could see they were peerin' down the necks of the empty milk bottles and pokin' in them with a bit of wire. I stood it as long as I could - then my curiosity got the better of me. 'Good evening,' I said. ''Ave you lost something?' 'Oh no,' one said, in a very la-di-da voice. 'We're lookin' for mice and field voles.' 'Serves me right,' I thought. 'Silly questions get silly answers.' But they weren't pulling my leg, they were genuine naturalists, professors or something at some university or other down London way and they were doing research on the small mammals that live in the countryside. You see, things like mice and voles are full of curiosity and they'll explore any hole they come across but when they do this and get into an empty milk bottle the glass is so slippery they can't get out so they die and provide a sort of sample of the small mammal population in the area for those who are busy researching such things.

The normal way of discovering how many animals there are is to set hundreds of traps to take a sample of the population but then someone discovered that owls and hawks eject pellets, like cigar butts, of indigestible food and if you pull them to pieces you can see what they've been feeding on by the bones they leave. Nature's way of sampling you might say.

A swarm of bees in June
Is worth a silver spoon.

June is one of the busiest months for bees. Did you know that one pound of honey is as good as thirty eggs or six pints of milk for energy? And to produce one pound of honey requires 40,000 individual loads of nectar, which may take up to 50,000 miles or twice round the world to gather? Depending of course, on how far the hive is from the flowers. Bees will work up to three miles away from base and may have to visit a hundred flowers to get one load of nectar.

There are a lot of superstitions about bees too, you know. They say they won't thrive if you quarrel about them, and if their owner dies, you have to 'tell' the hive and hang a piece of black crepe on it as a sign of mourning.

It's a wonderful month for bats too - there are several kinds of course, but the commonest is called the pipistrelle or flitter-mouse (flying-mouse, that is) and those are the ones you most often get in churches. Of course, they do make a certain amount of mess and smell, but they should be encouraged rather than chased out because they eat death watch beetles, so churches that are well batted are likely to have sounder timbers than ones where some local busybody has been at work. And you know, a bat chasing moths in a church roof can take your mind off a dull sermon and pass the time wonderfully - though our young vicar, Richard Adamson, doesn't very often preach dull ones I must say.

Our church is a great meeting place you know, with Dan and Laura being our churchwardens since I retired and Phil playing the organ - and we've got a good little band of bell-ringers now since we had the belfry repaired and the bells re-hung. You should come and have a look at it one day, very interesting, it is.

Some of you might think that a man like me who spends most of his life among trees might hardly notice them - 'can't see the wood for the trees' as the old saying goes. Or to turn it round the other way, 'can't see the trees for the wood!' Well, that's not true. I love a tree. And I'm not thinking of just any tree, but of one in particular. It's one of three old Scots pines that grows by themselves not far out of the village, on a byway off the road to Borchester. About twelve feet up the middle there's a hole where a branch was blown away, I don't know how many years ago; and in early summertime I always stops to see who's living there, because there's always some birds rearing a family in that hole.

A year or two back, and it was nuthatches who'd plastered the hole up with mud and clay to make the front door too small for bigger birds to get in. Lovely little bird, the nuthatch; it gets its name from its habit of hacking at nuts - hazel, beech, almond - to break them open. It has a pale blue beak with rusty pink underparts and a black stripe across its eye, and it's the only British bird that climbs down trees head first.

Well, two years it was nuthatches, and then came the tree-sparrows, cocky little birds they are with their black bibs and glossy brown caps. They was there for a year, and after them, when the nuthatches' front door had crumbled away, it was a pair of lesser spotted woodpeckers. Now it's starlings, gossiping, and screeching, and feeding a family just ready to come out into the world fatter than their parents. There's never a shortage of tenants in that old pine tree, and what a sight it is at sunset with its trunk in the golden light, and the bottle-green foliage. I could watch it for hours I can tell you - I love it.

But yesterday, I went bird-watching, not young pheasants but racing pigeons. You see this is the racing pigeon season and our Midland clubs were all busy racing. Now most people believe racing pigeons fly home by instinct from where they're let out and that they follow a straight line all the way. Well they don't - and yesterday I could see that for myself. You'll hardly believe it but they have recognised 'flight lines', a sort of main roads of the air and whole packs of them fly along these routes, often up valleys or below a line of hills, where the wind eddies help them instead of battering them back. Then when they get near home, they peel off the main flight line to do the last bit by local landmarks.

Well, yesterday afternoon I was up on Lakey Hill (up above Ambridge) looking over towards Borchester and I could see streams of birds coming up from down south. They was flying quite low along the valley and every now and then a little group, perhaps two or three, peeled out of the main stream over towards Penny Hassett and Layton Cross.

Now the pigeon that wins the race is not necessarily the one that gets home first, because some birds live further away than others and that wouldn't be fair, so it's won by the bird that flies home at the fastest average speed.

From where I was, high up on the hill, I could see the birds *below* me, flying where the wind had dropped, right down towards the floor of the valley. I've often watched the same sort of thing with swallows. When they come back from Africa, they don't fly the straightest line, they fly cunning, like those racing pigeons, making use of every scrap of help from nature.

Pigeon fliers know all about this, and I've even known a man who bought a house, not because of the view or because it was convenient for him to get to work, but because it was near a main flight line and *below* it. So when his birds were near home, they could fly the last few miles *down hill* while their rivals were battling over the crest to the next town! This may sound all very unlikely to you, but from where I was, I could see the birds actually doing it. There's tricks in every trade, isn't there?

Do you know if Prue 'ad offered me an egg for breakfast this morning, I'd almost have left her! I've seen so many eggs while I was keepering that there are times when I can't look one in the eye. You see, to a keeper spring and early summer *is* eggs. We collect pheasant's eggs for hatching, we hunt nests in dangerous places, like near stiles or footpaths, where they might be a temptation to ramblers' dogs as well as foxes and crows, we rescue eggs from nests in grass before it's cut for hay or silage, and hatch them in incubaters or under broody hens, and some keepers even buy eggs from game farms! So you'll understand when I say I sometimes feel as I've got eggs coming out of my ears! And yet although I've had too much of 'em, they still make me marvel. If you get an ordinary hen's egg and hold it between your hands, with an end sticking into each palm, you can't break it, however hard you press! As a matter of fact old Walter tried this once and his did bust all over his jacket! But that was only because it must have been cracked before he started. But in spite of its strength an egg-shell is porous. There's an air cell in the blunt end and as the chick develops it needs fresh air to sustain life and as it grows the air inside increases, until the egg will float in warm water if you put it in. Near to hatching, the chicks start to move and chip at the shell, which gradually gets more and more brittle until they can chip their way out.

The marvellous thing to me is that it may have taken the hen a fortnight or more to *lay* her clutch of eggs - but they all hatch out within a few hours of one another, and what makes them all hatch at the same time is that when one chick starts pecking at the shell and cheeping, it sets the others off too. The old broody hen hears them of course, and she chortles back so that for the last forty-eight hours or so, she hears the chicks and gets to know their voices - and they hear her and get to know hers. So when they do hatch, they recognise her as their mother, and they won't take any notice of any other hen, and she knows them as her chicks, even if she's an ordinary farmyard hen and they're pheasants!

Now guinea fowl, guinea fowls are different. They 'steal' nests in thickets which are very difficult to find. And if they are not found, they lay so many eggs that when they go broody, they often sit on a double layer of eggs so that as the eggs are moved in the nest, some are chilled, some are warm, and very few hatch. The easiest way to find the nest is to listen for the hen which makes a loud, high-pitched cackle whenever she finishes laying. You can then watch to see where she comes from. In fact guinea fowl are such noisy birds that they often shout and warn the world if they see a fox or a poacher, and countryfolk call them 'galeenies' because you see they are gallinacious birds related to turkeys and pheasants.

And talking about eggs and birds hatching out, have you ever wondered why little ducks swim and chickens don't? No, I'm not cadging silly answers to silly questions. It had never occurred to me either, until I saw a chap from the town nearly drown a lovely brood of ducklings the other day through sheer ignorance. You see, he'd bought these young ducklings, day-old white Aylesburys they was, and was rearing them with a broody hen. (A good broody hen, especially a bantam, will take to all sorts of young birds as a foster mother, keep them warm under her feathers and do a wonderful job rearing them. When I was a keeper, I used to rear pheasant, and wild duck, and partridge every year under broody hens.) Well, this chap's broody hen did all that was required of her but trying to be kind, the owner took the ducklings and put them in a steep sided bath of cold water for a swim. They loved it and swam round with such delight that he left them to it for an hour. That's where I came on the scene and he took me to show me how much they were enjoying themselves. But when we arrived they looked just like little submarines swimming under water with their periscopes sticking out. But what looked like periscopes was their little heads poking up and gasping for air. They was just on the point of sinking without trace and if they'd been left a few minutes more, they would have drowned.

Now if you put a chicken into water, you'd expect it to drown, not so much because it hasn't got webbed feet but because its down is so fluffy it would get waterlogged and sink. Well, these ducklings were just the same. They'd got waterlogged because they were being reared by a hen instead of a duck, because you see, a duck has an oil gland over its tail, just above the parson's nose and when she preens her feathers, she oils them from this gland. So when her little ducks brood under her, their down gets oily from the oily feathers of their mum and they can swim for a long time without getting wet, and bedraggled, and cold. But with these ducklings, their foster-mother couldn't oil them of course, and that nearly finished them off.

I wonder what some of you countryfolk - or townsfolk,

maybe - who've been out in the country around this time of the year thinks about haytime? Eh? Here in Ambridge we're in the thick of it just now. I'm not saying that one time of the summer's better than another, but I do say that for my money, haytime's near enough the best of it. First of all you've got the beauty of the hayfield before the cutters goes in, maybe with goldfinches, as bright as butterflies, flickering around the tops of some grasses which are more forward-seeding than others. Then when the grass is just right, juicy in the stalk and dry outside, out go the cutters behind the tractor and in a twink all the air smells green, and sappy, and sweet. No scent's sweeter to my way of thinking than the scent of new-mown hay, and sweeter still it smells after it's been laying there a while, and when the spreaders come like little wiry sideways-on cart-wheels to turn it over they just drench everything with the rich green perfume that's been storing itself up in there. Oh it's lovely!

They say too much looking back is not healthy but I'm not so sure about it. Haymaking when I was a lad - well, I reckon it looked prettier than it looks today, what with the swish-swish of the scythes through the sap, and the old hay-rakes coming after to ridge the mown grass - there'd be women in cotton sunbonnets with the hay-rakes and children romping in the hay and being told to stop. And there was something about the old pitchfork with its double tines, turning the hay and cocking it up before the horses came with the wain to cart it away.

The other night it was so beautiful that I was out late - one o'clock it was - and the silence was suddenly busted by a screamin' down in the wood as if someone was being murdered. The yellin' was louder than if a football team of tom cats had been stuffed into the same dustbin and although I've been brought up in game-keeping all my life, I've only heard that sound twice before. But there's nothing on earth like it, so I knowed what it was the second I heard it. It was badgers fightin'.

Old-fashioned keepers didn't like badgers because they have teeth like dogs and they couldn't believe they weren't harmful to game. But I don't mind them because if anything, they did my birds good by disturbing them if they roosted on the ground so that they flew up out of reach of foxes.

But although they're harmless to game and protected by law, badgers are anything but harmless to other badgers. They are very territorial too and if a strange badger comes into land belonging to another, the owner will chuck him out. And if the intruder doesn't want to go, they fight. And fight in earnest too. So I nipped up the wood with my spot lamp to see what was going on and they'd got stuck into it so much they didn't notice me. The one, the boss badger, had got his rival by the base of the tail and he was rippin' and shakin' him like a bull-terrier. But after a few seconds he noticed me and sloped off, and the other lay panned out on his tummy as if he was paralysed. It took him a long time to recover enought to get up and shuffle off and I reckon I arrived only just in the nick of time to save him.

But it's very rare for wild animals to fight to the death. They usually fight till one is proved boss and the loser runs away to fight another day. And very wise, too. But some domestic animals fight very seriously. Pigs for instance - and dogs, bulls and stallions too.

Prue wanted a few fresh dandelion leaves for a salad today, so she sent me out before breakfast to get them! Not that I minded of course, there's nothing like being first out in the country, whatever the weather. There wasn't much difficulty about finding them, it's been as bumper a harvest for them as it has for most wild flowers this year. But I went the long way round to make sure the chores were done when I got back and so I walked across the Lessurs to see how Phil's bunch of young heifers was coming on. Funny name, Lessurs, ain't it? Comes from the medieval name for pasture. Leasows it used to be. But then lots of fields have funny names, don't they? Half the pleasure of living in the country as opposed to visiting it is that you gradually get to know the origin of some of the local names.

Jackson's Croft, for instance, at the back of our house, had always defeated me. There isn't a Jackson anywhere around it could have been called after. And very few in the churchyard either! Then old Walter Gabriel just happened to mention quite casual one day, that his uncle had married a girl called

Jackson and that she gave her bridegroom the field as a wedding dowry - or rather her father did.

And right down at the edge of the wood below Arkwright Hall, there's a field called The Lawns. But don't run away with the idea that that was ever cut and rolled for croquet or tennis in the good old leisurely days, 'cos it wasn't. Centuries ago, a 'lawn' was just a clearing in a wood, when woods were often common land where the local villagers had the right to cut logs for burning, bracken for cattle bedding, to run pigs in autumn, and make clearings for hay in the winter. That's what a proper lawn was.

They were more romantic names then than calling a field 'the forty acre', or worse now I suppose, '16 point something or other hectares'! But my favourite of all was Bride's Hay. That was exactly what it said - where the local lads took their brides the first night they was wed.

I've been a bit irritable lately, because I've been wakened in the night and nagged all day lately, by the bleating of sheep. I wouldn't mind so much if it was the bleating of beautiful, plump comfortable looking sheep, but even the best of 'em look scraggy and miserable when they lose their fleeces. And the reason they look miserable is that even in an English summer, the nights are cool. If you'd had a woolly coat on for almost twelve months you'd feel the chill of even a June night, whatever they say about casting your clout when May is out - whether by that they mean the May flower or the month.

But shearing here on lowland English farms is very different from the job where Pat Archer comes from in Wales. The sheep run wild on the hills there, instead of in enclosed fields where they're easy to drive and pen. And when I say the Welsh sheep are wild, I mean *wild.* So the Welsh farmers make a proper do of it. A real neighbourly do. When one is ready, they all gang up with their sheep dogs and drive everything off together. And those Welsh border collies are as sure-footed as antelopes, and as tough as athletes, and on top of that, they are so in tune with what their masters want that they make me believe in telepathy. They can fetch, and gather, and drive, and pen, and single out, at the sound of a whistle just like an act in a circus - extraordinary they are.

Prue and I have an old honeysuckle - rather a late one - that's just over its full blooming and of a June evening when it fills the whole garden with its sweet scent, then the moths come to it, hawkmoths in particular, though not so many as there used to be. But other moths, too - and I've heard the midsummer dusk called 'the moth hour' - there's a lovely name for you.

But best of all to me at the end of a summer's day is the swifts, racing on their dark, thin wings over the village, then up into the sky - higher and higher till they're out of sight. They say they sleep on the wing - I wonder. I wouldn't be surprised, because swifts really do belong to the sky - really are part of it, as you might say. And of a midsummer's night they just disappear into it. Devil Birds some calls them - but I'd say they're more the other thing, because they're always heading for heaven of a night-time in June ... that's one of the reasons why I love the month so much.

July

Sweet summer time when the leaves are green and long.

Although it was pretty hot I said I'd help Gordon out the other day by popping over to Borchester with a tractor and trailer for a load of pheasant food he wanted. You can get special pheasant rearing crumbs you know, but they're very expensive, so he uses the pellets they make for chickens which are cheaper and seem just as good. And they put vitamins, and antibiotics and all sorts of clever stuff in 'em to make the birds grow fast and prevent disease, so they're a bargain in their way.

I love driving along the roads on a tractor on a fine day. The seat is perched so high you can look down over the hedges into peoples' gardens, but Martha Woodford's washing looked so white that I was afraid a smut would blow out of my exhaust - which sticks up like a chimney on a tractor - and leave a trademark she'd be able to trace to me, so I hurried on. And I must remember to tell old Walter the spuds he reckoned escaped that late frost wouldn't look so good in an aerial photograph if he had one taken. And I saw odd nooks and corners in some folks' gardens that I never knew was there. And lovely flowerbeds belongin' to folks I'd allus thought wouldn't know a weed from a wasp.

It's surprising what a difference it makes to the view too being up on a tractor. Just that few feet higher seemed to bring Borchester next door as you might say, when hedges would have made it like a hundred miles away if I'd been on foot or in a car.

And a tractor's better than a psychologist for showing up folks' characters! If I'm in a car and get bogged down behind a tractor it makes me fume! But sitting up on my own at the head of the queue's another matter. I can't see what all the rip and tear's about then. Time doesn't matter any more, because although a tractor snorts and rattles a bit, it takes you back and reminds you of more leisurely days when country folk drove horses and traps. 'Course, horses smelt sweeter than tractors and there wasn't any sound nicer than the clip-clop of the hooves coming up the lane. And you could see your friend coming half a mile away and you knew there was time for him to stop and have a chat instead of roarin' past before he'd had time to recognise you.

There's a bit of that spirit in the country even today, you know. Some folks still have time to cook real country dishes and time to learn real country skills like thatchin' and hedge layin' and important things like that.

Summer's lease hath all too short a date.

I was mindin' my business the other day, walking along a lane when I noticed the cattle over the hedge. There they all were quietly browsing, or chewing the cud of what they'd already browsed, just as if tomorrow would do for anything. Then without any warning, up went their tails and they charged off down the field like a regiment of soldiers. It brought me to me cake and milk, I tell you. I thought at first that some strange customer was trying a short cut - and letting his dog out for a walk at the same time. Young beasts will often chase a strange dog and they can be very dangerous too, not by tossing him in anger so much, as by trampling him underfoot in the stampede. So I got over the fence but there was nobody there. The cattle was 'gadding', that's what is was. Now you may not know what that is, but this is the time of year when the gadflies, or clegs, are at their worst, especially if the weather turns a bit on the thundery side. They're not as bad as warble-flies because they don't do so much damage to hides, which are often ruined by warbles even with modern chemical dressings. But gadflies are bad enough. Proper fierce blood suckers they are, and they make a loud droning sound when they're flying. As alarming to cows as an air raid siren is to us I reckon. And the men among you won't be surprised to hear that it's the female flies that make the noise - and are the fiercest!

When cattle hear that drone, they ups with their tails and panics round the field trying to escape from the painful bites. That's where the expression 'gadding about' came from, I suppose.

And horses are even worse at gadding than cattle. They're more panicky for one thing, and they've got thinner hides. I remember one year I'd reared a grand bunch of goslings which was grazing with the old geese in a paddock behind our cottage. Well, the gadflies started off a few quiet ponies going round the field like the Charge of the Light Brigade and they galloped straight over my goslings and killed the two biggest of 'em. So I've always had a grudge against gadflies - and you can't blame me, can you!

I wonder if any of you are keen fishermen? I daresay a lot are, for it seems to me about this time of year that half the world's gone fishing-crazy, and you notice it in a place like Ambridge - not that our river's a big one, so folk take a day off from time to time and drive off to bigger ones - away in the morning early and not back much afore midnight if they've made what they calls a 'real day of it'. Oh, yes, they'll drive fifty miles or more to get good fishing - and pay a lot for it if it's in one of the big reservoirs or on a stretch of river where the game-fish are - trout and grayling, and maybe if they're lucky, the odd salmon.

It's a wonderful relaxation though is fishing - not that I've ever been a great one for it myself. Always seem to find that there's something more important needs doing. Or is it more important? I wonder - a day by the waterside can do more good to a man than worrying himself about something that - well - will keep till tomorrow.

You know one of the nice things about living in the country is the bit of land that goes with most houses. Our cottage isn't very grand and the plumbing isn't as good as it might be and there are potholes in the lane, but think of the advantages! The honeysuckle up the porch perfumes the whole house on summer evenings and great elephant hawk moths come there for the nectar on still nights.

There's a patch of garden at the front where Prue grows cottagey flowers like roses, lavender and violets. She likes flowers that smell sweet or are billiant in colour, like geraniums, or the ones that attract butterflies such as michaelmas daisies.

When we get back from work at night and we've had our tea, we do an hour's pottering in the garden - in the bit where we grow the vegetables.

It's a wonderful feeling to let fertile soil run through your fingers. When a garden has been dug, and forked, and raked and mucked for years, the soil gets that lovely crumbly texture that gives gardeners as much pleasure as a carpenter gets when he strokes a piece of furniture made by an old craftsman centuries ago.

And digging isn't the hard work you might think - when you understand how to dig and the soil's been turned over so often it almost comes up to meet you!

And afterwards it's wonderful to pop round to The Bull and boast over a pint, about the peas, and the beans, and spuds we've had for nothing, while others have to buy theirs - and they cost a pretty penny nowadays, don't they?

The English winter—ending in July,
To recommence in August.

Well, Lord Byron, the poet, said that, but he was wrong really because although traditionally July (called after Julius Caesar) is a wet month, it can be a very hot one too and it can often be thundery and it's a very silent month for bird song. This is because most of the nesting is finished and the birds' plumage has got to its worst state of the year, so the old feathers are dropped or moulted, and the birds are very sore and miserable in consequence. Some birds, ducks, swans and geese in particular, moult so quickly that they lose so many of the main flight feathers from their wings that they can't fly at all for a couple of weeks or so, and they have to congregate on reservoirs and other large sheets of water where they can swim to the middle and be safe from their enemies.

But one of the very few birds to sing this month is the nightjar or goatsucker. It makes a continuous churring noise rather like a finger drawn across the teeth of a comb and it usually starts about dusk. It used to be believed by Aristotle and people like that, that they sucked the udders of goats and sent them blind. They have a lot of other names too such as fern-owl, moth-eater and gabble-ratch, and the Danes call them helrakke, or death hound, while in Shropshire they're a lich-fowl or corpse-fowl. But in fact they are harmless and delightful birds and the only odd thing they do is sit *along* branches instead of across them!

It's getting on time now for the swifts to migrate back to Africa - and it's extraordinary, because when the young ones fledge and leave the nest, they don't go back to it but set off without any training or a guide, straight for Africa, and young ones which have been marked have been recovered there within a few days of leaving their nests in England - and nobody knows yet how they find their way.

Turtle doves are still cooing but they'll soon be off to Africa too. Starling and lapwings (or peewits) are beginning to flock and the rooks and herons have left their breeding grounds. And if you were to look at the wild duck down by Arkwright Hall lake you'd think they was all female, because the drakes have moulted out of their brilliant breeding plumage and won't be showing it again till autumn.

And talking of birds, I was walkin' through one of our woods the other day early, before six o'clock, and when I came to the edge of the trees I stood still to take stock and I noticed a stranger crouching by a patch of thistles. And I couldn't think what he was watching. I thought at first perhaps there was a rabbit squattin' in a tussock and that he was getting ready to pounce on it and if he had I should have pounced on him and copped him red-handed. But he never stirred a muscle, so I moved quietly up behind him and he never noticed me till I was towerin' above him and said 'Good morning, you seem interested.' He nearly jumped out of his skin. 'Now look what you've done,' he said. 'You've frightened them off.' 'Frightened what off?' I said. 'Why, them seven-coloured linnets I was watching. Feedin' on thistle heads they were. A holiday's not a holiday without seein' some seven-coloured linnets.' He was very annoyed, he was. It's a lovely name for a lovely bird, isn't it - seven-coloured linnets? The proper name that ornithologists use is goldfinch, but it's not half so nice, is it?

So if you get out in the country at this time of year and keep your eyes skinned, the chances are that you will see a charm of goldfinches - or seven-coloured linnets - feeding on ripe thistle heads for the seeds. They're about as big as sparrows and they really are brilliant with red, and black, and white on the head and yellow splashes on the wings. Then they've got buff, and tawny, and pale yellows too which make them among the most gorgeous birds I know.

I enjoyed talking to this stranger because he was calling the birds by their country names which are much prettier than the ones the posh chaps use. His chaffinches were 'pie finches' because of the white or pied bar on their wings; sparrows were 'spuggocks' and greenfinches 'Joeys'. I'd misjudged him when I thought he might be a poacher because he works in a factory all the year but always goes bird watchin' for his holidays - and he does nobody any harm at all.

Have you noticed all the bees on the lavender bushes in July, and on the golden agrimony that used to be used by old cottagers as 'tea'? There are lots of weeds about too - milkweed, thistle, wild carrot and shepherd's purse - and then there's the clover. And, of course, the pimpernel with its crimson petals - that used to be known as the poor man's weather glass or the shepherd's clock, because it closes up before rain. It's supposed to close at noon and never opens before seven o'clock in the morning. And there are blue forget-me-nots about, red poppies, marigolds, sunflowers, night-scented stock, foxgloves, hollyhocks, Canterbury bells and the buddleia which attracts so many butterflies - red admirals and peacocks - Oh, I could go on and on. But it's such a wonderful month for country smells too, ranging from the sweet honeysuckle to sharp pungent mint and the coarse scent of elderberry which often grows near a badger sett, and that is because badgers are such splendid diggers that there is always a pile of fine tilth soil which is ideal to germinate the elderberries carried by birds.

St Swithin's day, if thou dost rain,
For forty days it will remain;
St Swithin's day, if thou be fair,
For forty days 'twill rain nae mair.

But you'll know all about St Swithin I'm sure - 15 July that's his day - but do you know about two other old country superstitions? One is that to see the old moon in the arms of the new is a sign of fair weather and the other is that if after death the corpse doesn't stiffen, there'll be another death in the family before the end of the year.

There used to be a great deal of nail-biting among our farmers in case there was a lot of rain this month - but not so much now. You see up till the last war before there were the big combine harvesters, the corn had to be cut before it was quite ripe, and then allowed to ripen in the stook. So it was cut by binders which spewed out the sheaves tied together by binder twine. Then those had to be gathered and 'stooked' in rows, which were dried by the air until completely ripe. When they were ready they were collected and carried away by waggons or tractor trailers and made into ricks - and of course, there was a lot of waste grain at each stage, and bad weather before it was in could be a real disaster, but now with combine harvesters, the corn is allowed to get much riper, and even if it gets wet modern corn driers can usually prevent it from going mouldy. But for wildlife the old way was best, because the grain that got dropped was food for partridge and pheasant, and lots of smaller birds.

The foxes have lairs and the
birds of the air their nests...

The fox cubs that were born in March as a result of that mating I told you about, will often move out of the fox 'earth' this month and make thick couches in the standing corn before it's cut or in the late hay. This is partly 'camping out' in the hot weather, but it's also a good way of getting deloused after sharing the 'earth' with so many others. They play around and can flatten quite large areas as badger cubs do but a single thunderstorm can flatten far more corn than all the cubs in the district, so most farmers are ready to put up with them. However when the corn is cut, you quite often see a litter of fox cubs who haven't been far enough from the 'earth' to know anywhere else, so when they're disturbed, they're quite lost and don't know what to do.

And talking about cubs, last night I went out for a stroll to cool off and, as I often do, I watched out for badger cubs - they're as big as cats by now and as playful as puppies - and as bold as brass, 'cos they haven't learned anyone can wish them any harm yet. Now although I spent so many years as a gamekeeper, I don't dislike badgers, because on balance I believe they do more good than harm. Anyhow the cubs I was watching was a delight, and they chattered and rolled each other down the bank below the sett as if they was having a real fight, and not a mock battle at all. Their hair stuck out stiff as a frightened cat's tail to make 'em look bigger and fiercer than they were and when they got really excited, the still summer air was filled with a powerful, musky pong. Now this scent, which is produced from a special gland under their tail, is very important to badgers. They're so short sighted that they find their way home by following their own trail of smell.

And they use it like a skunk to warn off enemies too. And most important of all, they use it to mark out their own territory and warn other badgers to keep off - so that musky pong of theirs has a lot of uses.

I was over in Borchester last market day and ran into a pal I hadn't seen for all of five years. 'Why, Tom,' he says, 'you haven't changed a bit since I see you last - same old Tom.' 'Come to that,' says I, 'same goes for you, Fred - same old Fred. What about a pint for old times' sake, eh? What was that pub you used to go to just outside the town?' 'Ah,' says he, 'you mean The Green Dragon.' He asked if I'd been in there lately, and I said, 'No, it must be all of a twelvemonth.' 'You'll not recognise the place,' says he, 'but the beer's still good.'

Not recognise the place! He was right enough there. You never saw the like. The Dragon used to be a nice, simple old-fashioned sort of pub and old Peter Potts what kept it an old-fashioned landlord. But now - well, I couldn't believe my eyes. They'd turned one of the rooms into someone's idea of an Austrian beer hall, with stag's heads everywhere and the beer served in pint-pots with lids on 'em. Even the taproom was tricked out with bean-hooks, mattocks and other old country working tools. That wasn't too bad, but the lounge, what used to be an old saloon bar - copper bar-tops, hunting horns, a carpet with a John Peel design on it and curtains to match and the lighting so dim as you couldn't see your beer and music so loud you couldn't hear yourself speak.

Now I'm not one to stand in the way of progress but this mix-up wasn't so much progress as - well, I thought it had all gone a bit too far. Old Peter Potts wasn't there either but a young manager chap with bushy whiskers. Give me Sid and Polly and the dear old Bull. Even if it has changed a bit, it's changed 'for real' as they say.

I reckon the last time I had something to tell you about cricket was when Netherbourne and Penny Hassett was playing their end-of-the-season match last year. Now it's the new season and I'm glad to say as cricket's really got going again in Ambridge. I'm not quite what you'd call a youngster, but there's plenty of really old chaps here in the village - chaps as used to play in their leather belts and braces - and to hear them talking as they sits watching a game is a real treat. 'Call that fast?' says one to another, as Harry Booker was trundling them down at a fair old pace to my way of thinking. 'Why,' the old chap goes on, 'I reckon as Ted Sparrow was twice as fast as this feller.' 'Ted Sparrow,' says his mate, 'he really *was* fast. He could have played for the county if he'd had a mind to.'

And, of course, when it comes to watching today's batsmen there's not one of them as would have rated a place in the Ambridge side of 1922! And off the old chaps goes again with: 'Remember Ron Moffit? There was a rare clouter for you, was Ron. I seen him hit four in a row over the oak tree. But these chaps today ... pat-ball, that's all they does.'

Well it so happened as I got hold of a score-book more than fifty years back just to have a look as to *how* good those 'giants of yesterday' really was. Seems as the great 'clouter' Ron Moffit hit just one six in the whole season of 1920; he was out 'hit wicket' four times in three matches, his highest score was twenty-one, and his average for the season was eight! As for the 'demon bowler' Ted Sparrow, well, when I tell you that he was no-balled four times in a single match, and sent down seven wides you'll agree as he wasn't exactly county class! Of course I never let on to the old chaps, I just let them go on dreaming of the 'giants of yesterday'!

And talking of old times do you remember the old fairs that used to come to country villages in the summer? I don't mean the big noisy ones with all sorts of smelly machines but the rare old country fairs. Just a handful of travelling folk with half-a-dozen stalls selling trinkets, and printed cottons, and 'bunches of blue ribbons', I dare say for some maid to tie around her bonny brown hair! There'd be a man with an armful of puppies for sale, and once I remember there was a dancing dog, and a stall for the kiddies - Dutch dolls, balloons, little celluloid windmills on sticks and that. But, of course, what we nippers liked best was the candy stall. There'd be an old woman dipping apples into a pan of thin, bubbly toffee with one hand, while she pulled thick hot toffee from a big lump of it wrapped around a sort of metal contraption with the other. And, of course, peppermint rock - there always had to be peppermint rock. But that was all long ago, though we still sometimes gets morris men from Borchester dancing on our village green and working up a rare old thirst. They come dancing for the sheer love of it - dressed all in white, with coloured sashes, and bells strapped to their knees, and a fiddler playing, and a chap on the accordion. They have the hobby-horse with them, and the fool with his bladder chasing the kids. And it seemed as the Borchester morris men, and other teams from round and about, had been dancing through the villages all day, and were all meeting up in Hollerton for the evening. And I likes to see these chaps, young and old, enjoying theirselves - and there's nothing 'cissy' about it, I can tell you, it's real hard work. Old war-dances of the Spanish Moors they come from, so I'm told.

Out in our Deer Park at this time of year, the fallow bucks will be 'fraying' off the velvet of their antlers ready for the rut in October. You see the bucks cast, or drop, their mature antlers before the fawns are born in June, sometimes as early as the beginning of May, and the new set grow in about fourteen weeks, and while they are growing they are quite soft, and they're supplied with blood by a rough, soft outer covering rather like velvet and by July, although still soft, they are often fully formed, being 'in velvet' we call it. Now you see, the early bucks will 'fray' off this velvet against the branches of bushes and saplings and sometimes they'll do this about the beginning of the month - and when they've done it we call them 'clean' because the hard bone is exposed and polished by this 'fraying'. Now these bucks, they have to grow what amounts to several pounds of solid bone in fourteen weeks or so, and to do this they have to have a lot of calcium and phosphates. They get some of it by eating the old cast-off antlers, and make up as much of the rest as they can from any suitable foodstuffs they can find - surprising, isn't it?

The other evening there I was out in our bit of garden when I heard what sounded like someone with a terrible heavy 'summer cold'. It was coming from the compost heap in the corner, and I knew it was something as no old ex-gamekeeper should have a great fancy for. But when that old hedgehog came snuffling over the grass towards me, tame as you please and not afraid of anything - why, I hadn't it in my heart not to call out to Prue - 'Bring us a saucer of milk, love - we got a visitor.' It didn't take him three minutes to find where that saucer was - and Prue and I watched him snouting and snuffling about till it was clean. And I daresay next time we see him - or her, as it might be - there'll be a litter of babies, size of ping-pong balls, being shown the world. Just so long as mother has had the good sense not to go out in the road and get in the way of a car. A dead hedgehog in the road - that's a thing I don't like, but mind you, I don't blame the motorist - it's not his fault.

And then the other morning on the edge of the estate I suddenly heard a noise as loud as a forest fire crackling, and whatever it was seemed to have asthma, it was wheezin', and snufflin', and breathin' so loud, but it turned out to be nothing more than another hedgehog - and this one was hunting snails.

You see hedgehogs love snails and beetles, and if you could have heard him crunch those snail-shells, you'd understand why they call him hedge-*hog*! And if you looked at him close as I did, you'd see he has a snout like a hog, too!

Now that morning up there, it was so quiet except for the

hedgehog, you could hear the grasshoppers fiddling away like a string quartet as soon as there was a bit of warmth in the sun and the hover-flies made as much row as Prue's old sewing machine. A few yards from the hedge there was an old cow lying down chewing the cud. Terrible manners she had, for she kept belching. Then she'd start chewing with a rhythm that was so loud I couldn't understand why I'd never noticed it before. As I was thinking about it, the old hedgehog shuffled up and began to lick the drops of milk that had shed from her udder. He didn't touch the cow, he'd have prickled her if he had, he just licked the drops from the grass as delicate as a cat, and I reckon as that explains the old wives' tale about hedgehogs milking cows, don't you?'

August

And with his sickle keen
He reaps the bearded grain,
And the flowers that grow between.

Of course, August is harvest month - it didn't used to be but modern methods has changed things. You see, the combine harvester can take the corn almost completely ripe, whereas in the old days using a binder a great deal of grain would have to be shed and lost at this time of year.

But now I'll tell you about something else for a moment, and that's wild oats. D'you know there's more of that about in Ambridge this summer than there are spines on a hedgehog? Mind you I'm not casting aspersions on old Walter - and don't get any ideas about me, because I gave up sowing my wild oats longer ago than I care to think about. No, the wild oats in Ambridge was real ones, not the sort old-fashioned school gaffers was always preaching about. Now the funny thing is, that then nobody ever complained much about wild oats in their corn because they were pretty rare. It's only in modern times they've become a pest and to be honest I've never seen as many about as there are this year. There's no mistaking them - they stand head and shoulders above the other crops, so you can see a lovely level crop of golden wheat or barley, and waving six or eight inches above it what looks like very good oats - but really they're shading the crop of corn, and stealing it's food too. But you know, in a way you've got to admire the wild oat for its persistence. You see it produces fifty or so seeds from each head, and instead of all these growing the next year some of them lie dormant in the soil for years on end. It's like the old saying - 'one year's seeding is seven years weeding' - and once you've got 'em, your problem just goes on getting worse and worse!

Of course it didn't happen when I was young because we always used to rotate the crops, and have roots and grass after corn, so the wild oats didn't get a chance of getting a hold. But now they grow corn time after time on the same land, they have to use expensive sprays and even 'rogue' out the survivors by hand - and that's a long and tiresome job, that is.

You sun-burn'd sicklemen of August weary...

Well they've broken the back of the harvest round here now but looking back it's astonishing how things have changed. For instance, my grandfather was born long before corn was harvested by machines. In his time they cut it with scythes and gangs of men used to go round the country living at whichever farm they was working on. Eight or ten men would work in a line and all you could hear was the rhythmic shuffling of the scythes felling the corn in swathes. They were followed by gangs of women and kids tying it into sheaves with plaited straw.

They still harvest like that in some parts of Ireland and once when I went over to size up some salmon fishing Mr Woolley thought of renting, I marvelled that time had stood still for so long, but with such little fields and so much stone, machines wouldn't be possible there really, so what else can they do?

Of course by my time, they'd finished cutting corn with scythes here, and we used to harvest it with horses and a binder. I loved the smell of those horses and the rattle of the binder as it 'spitted' sheaves out in rows ready for us to stack up in stooks to dry. And then later on, we had to unstack them and pitch them onto waggons to be carted to the stackyard where we built them into tidy ricks.

There were rabbits to chase in the corn and later in the winter rats to catch in the stackyard. Yes, harvest involved much more manual labour in those days, but it was such skilled labour that it made you feel proud when the neighbours came along to harvest supper. And although it was sweaty dusty work, it was done at a more leisurely pace, so there was always time for a bit of sport and a swig of cider while the horses had a breather. I think in some ways everything's too clever by half these days and we've lost a lot of the joy and pleasure in things. Mind you, there are still some lovely sights about. I saw one this morning - a trail of gypsy caravans, makin' for Evesham way for fruit picking, I suppose. Or workin' their way down to Hereford or Worcester for hop-pickin' time and what I liked was that they weren't in motor lorries piled up with junk, but proper gypsies like there were when I was a kid. Brown as berries with black hair and laughing. But, of course, with motors instead of horses.

They'd got some lovely lurchers with 'em too - big running dogs like greyhounds but with rough, hairy coats like collies. Proper lurchers, the real ones, were originally produced by crossing greyhounds with collies, you know. That gave them the speed of the runner and the toughness of the collie. And more important than toughness, they was as intelligent and cunning as their masters.

You might think that having been a keeper, I ought to hate lurchers, because they have been poachers' dogs for generations. But you can respect real professional skill even in a rival, can't you? Besides they usually only took what they wanted to eat - not like these thugs as drive round in motor cars with rifles. Hit-and-runners, who take a pot-shot and sneak off. I hate them.

But way back before I was a keeper, I was great pals with an old gypsy. I used to go out with him as a lad, I did. We knew every gap in every hedge for miles around. It's true as they say you can't be a good keeper without knowin' how to be a good poacher too!

Anyhow this old gypsy, Cornelius they called him, he had a wonderful lurcher bitch called Smoke. She knew what she was doing all right. If there was a stranger about she'd slip through the hedge and disappear so there was no suspicion we was poaching with a dog. And she wouldn't come back till the coast was clear. If she caught a rabbit or a hare, she'd sneak off back to the van with it so he wouldn't be caught with incriminating evidence. Or if Cornelius gave a low whistle, she'd retrieve it like a spaniel - and go and catch another. You couldn't say she was a good house dog because she always lay up under the caravan, but she was a wonderful guard and like a mother to all the kids, Smoke was.

You know, seeing that string of vans and gypsy folk brought back my boyhood to me. Got me quite sentimental it did. And though it may sound daft, if they'd slipped a dog into one of Mr Woolley's fields and picked up a hare for their dinner, I think I'd have looked the other way!

The Glorious Twelfth, eh? The day the grouse-shooting season opens. I've never had much to do with grouse of course, because most of my keepering was done in wooded lowlands, so you can understand I was very pleased when a pal invited me to have a look round the grouse moor where he works in Yorkshire a year or two back.

There's tricks in every trade they say, but I don't think I'd like his job somehow. Instead of a nice little cottage, sheltered and handy for the village, like where Prue and I live, he lives at the back of beyond in an old shepherd's hut, miles up a track over the moor. It's so windy there that the trees are all lop-sided, and his water is piped from a spring up in the hills.

The view's all right, sky and rolling hills, but you can't live on fresh air and view, can you? It's trees and shade that I'd miss. He says the wind goes straight through you in the winter. And I believe him!

Of course, in many ways his job is the same as mine was. We both had to see our birds had plenty of food and plenty of nesting cover. And no interference from foxes, crows and such like, or from people for that matter.

My pheasants and partridges liked corn, seeds, berries and insects. His grouse want heather - and you'd think that'd be easy, wouldn't you? There's nothing but heather for as far as you can see on those moors. But grouse are funny birds. They don't just want any old heather, it must be tender young heather. They're mighty particular, grouse are.

So my pal has to spend time every year burning off patches of heather so there is always some young stuff for eating, and some old for nesting. And he rotates his patches round like farmers used to their crops. But it's a hair-raising job picking just the right wind and the right weather, so his fires don't get out of hand and burn off more than he means to. And there's another thing too - his moor's so peaty there isn't enough grit for his birds' digestion, so he has to put piles of it along the tracks for them. It may be worth it to him, but I'd sooner spend the twelfth of August in the woods round Ambridge than up on that wild windswept moor with him, I can tell you.

And talking of it being August, I forgot to tell you that it's called after the Roman Emperor, Augustus, who thought it was his lucky month. I don't know whether he was very superstitious or not, but did you know in the country they used to say it's unlucky to kill a pig in the wane of the moon and if you do, it'll waste in the boiling? And here's another one - did you know it's unlucky to go into a house you're going to live in by the back door? And another - and this one is for fishermen - if you count what you've taken you won't catch any more!

Now, what was I on about before I started telling you those old superstitions? Oh yes, grouse-shooting. Well, people like

Mr Woolley may go up north for a few days on the moors, but they don't have to go all the way to Scotland, because some of the best shooting is in Yorkshire where my old pal is, and in the Pennines in Staffordshire. But more and more people are grouse-hawking now rather than shooting. It's a spectacular business but it's very expensive because top class falcons can fetch up to £1,000 for gyrs and several hundreds from home bred peregrines - and of course, this led last year to half the peregrines' nests, which are called 'eyries', being robbed.

All their desire is in the work of their craft.

We had our village fête as usual this year and I forgot to tell you about it, but as we had a new stall there, I'm going to now. Local crafts, it was - and very popular too. You know the sort of thing - the Women's Institute did tapestries, and pillow-cases and tea-towels, and folks who had been to evening classes in Borchester had done some lovely leatherwork. But what took my fancy was the walking-sticks. I've been interested in making my own sticks all my life. Of course, having been a keeper, always about in woodland gives me great advantages, so I look at trees from two quite different points of view! I see the lovely colours and shapes, that everybody else sees, and then I look at each branch separately to decide just where to cut the blanks, that with a few hours work on winter nights can be made into fine walking-sticks.

Nut trees, hazelnuts, make lovely thumb-sticks for example, and when I see a young shoot, no thicker than my little finger, forking at about the right height, I often prune the branches round it to give it space to grow. Then I watch it for two or three years till it's exactly the right size and shape for cutting.

I've got an old bathtub of moist sand which I heat on an old camping gas-ring and I bury the blank sticks in the sand till they're pliable so I can bend hook-handles or straighten out kinks I don't want. And when they're just right, I leave them to season and grow into money better than in the bank! A very good sideline, walking-sticks were.

So, of course, I look at trees as far more than the raw

material for fencing-posts, or planks, or logs to burn. And I like some of the by-products too. Ivy for instance. There used to be those who cut any ivy they found growing up trees in a wood, because they said it was a parasite and strangled them, some still say that. But the Forestry Commission don't mind it - and they should know! They say ivy only uses trees as a support to climb up and it gets all its food from its roots in the ground. Honeysuckle does far more damage because it clings so tight it really will strangle small trees. But I often wind honeysuckle round a hazel twig or bit of blackthorn deliberately. Then as it grows, the twig gets a lovely spiral groove right round the stem which makes a lovely original walking-stick - there's tricks in every trade as I've said before!

Prue made such a lot of mushroom chutney last time that she'd still got a couple of dozen jars left, so she sent them round to the fête. Funny things mushrooms, they spread underground especially in hot weather. You see they thrust out tendrils called mycellium and then when the autumn rains come (as they always do in time) the fruiting bodies, that's the mushrooms, shoot up from their underground runners. Well, in dry weather like some we've had, the runners go well, but the ground has been baked so hard recently that the mushrooms have a job to get through to the surface at all. But the slots cut for the seeds of direct sown turnips are just what they need. So, in the turnip and kale fields round here, there are sometimes rows of lovely natural field mushrooms in every slot - and we often have quite a few popping up haphazard in the turf fields, like they always used to in my young days at the bottom end of June.

Forth issuing on a summer's morn
Among the pleasant villages and farms...

Of course, we're in the very thick of holiday time now, and I reckon as Ambridge isn't the only village as notices it. Not that we're exactly a 'holiday resort' but now everything is so expensive, it seems to me as more and more folks are taking their holidays just pottering around the byways of the countryside, stopping to consult their maps, looking at sign-posts, and wondering just where to go from here.

It's the 'How's the best way to get to Midchester from here?' business as makes me laugh sometimes if I drops into The Bull for a drink at dinner-time. You see, there's not a pub anywhere I reckon as hasn't got its arguefiers when it comes to trying to help strangers on their 'best ways,' and managing atween them to get the poor folks more lost than ever.

'Midchester?' says someone, 'your best way out of here's to take the Penny Hassett Road, go on a couple of miles out of the village where ye'll see the road forks by a Dutch barn - now you takes the left fork and carries on, straight as you can go till you come to a T-junction - there you goes left for about a mile on the Darrington road and you'll see a line of poplars...'

'Now, look here, Dave,' says somebody else, 'what do they want to go all around Darrington way for? Midchester lies west o' Borchester, not east, don't it? If I was you, sir - now, let's see that map of yours - there now, your best way's to take the right turn afore you gets to Penny Hassett - see? Just keep going till you come to a post-mill on your left-hand side, see - now just past that post-mill...'

'You're both daft,' says some other know-all, 'best way o' getting to Midchester's by way of what they used to call the 'Old Coach Road' - more of a track than a road - lays out of Netherbourne...'

Then, of course, someone else says: 'Bit out of date aren't you, mate? Been ploughed up this past five years...'

And there's the poor holidaymakers wishing as they'd kept their mouths shut and never thought of coming out at all.

Wasps? August and September are about the worst months for wasps. Now I'll tell you something. When old Walter was a boy, they used to go after wasps' nests with a length of fuse, the sort miners used for 'blowing' coal in the mines, or woodmen used for 'blowing' tree stumps. What they did was this. First they had to locate the nest and mark it by day, which they did either by watching where the wasps went or by catching one and tying a bit of coloured wool round its waist - of course this slowed down its flight as well so you could see where it went. Then after dark when they'd all be inside, you knotted a length of fuse so it could be pushed down the entrance tunnel of the nest, but you had to light the end of the fuse before you pushed it in. Well, it fizzed and smoked like a firework, and when you'd got it right down the hole you covered it all up with a spadeful of earth to keep the smoke in. You took ten minutes off for a pint at the local to let the wasps become stupefied by the smoke, and then you dug the nest out. It was like a paper football with thousands of grubs in what looked a bit like a honeycomb, though of course, wasps feed the grubs on flies and things, not honey. And the advantage of using a fuse and not poison gas is that the grubs are not harmed and can be used as bait when you go fishing. But, of course, if you stopped in the pub for a second pint and air had leaked into the nest, the wasps might have recovered from the smoke and you'd get a shirtful of stings!

Now while I'm on about wasps I'll tell you something else. When I was coming back home out of the wood the other day, I noticed a hollow in the hedgebank about the size of a football. Freshly scooped out it was, as neat and round as if it had been done with a big ice-cream scoop. Well I looked a bit closer, and it was obvious it had been a wasp nest, and about a yard away there was quite a lot of papery crust that the nest had been built in and fragments of the comb too. Like a honeycomb, it was, but it'd had grubs, the wasp larvae, in it instead of honey of course. Now although badgers love honey, they love wasp grubs more, and I could see that this nest had been dug out by a badger. You see, when badgers are wandering along quietly at night, I think they hear the buzzing in wasp nests, as well as smelling the grubs, so they dig the nest out and eat them. I've seen eight holes already this year where the badgers have been doin' a wonderful job catchin' them before they grow up and get too bad with the fruit. But I'll admit this - in my life keepering I saw literally hundreds of hollows where wasps' nests had been dug out by badgers, but if you asked me how they dig 'em out without getting stung - I couldn't tell you. Badgers has got wonderful thick hides, of course. I wouldn't argue about that. And when they fluff out their fur, like a cat's tail when she's being chased by a dog, I'm sure the wasps haven't stings long enough to get to the skin. That may have something to do with it.

Now when I was a kid, I had a tame hand-reared badger as a pet. It's illegal to keep them as pets now, and quite right, because so few people can give then enough liberty. But my badger would follow me round like a dog, and he came for a walk every night with me, and I happened to know where there was a wasp nest in a bank, so we went in that direction, and when we got near it I stood still, and let him forage about.

Sure enough, he found the nest almost at once, and although he had never seen one before he knew what it was and got very excited and his fur stood out round him as stiff as a chimney-sweep's brush. Then he started to dig and the turf flew out in tussocks and wasps buzzed round him in a swarm but with no effect because they couldn't get to his skin.

But when he started to eat the grubs it was a different story. His mouth and tongue had no hairs round, and the wasps soon nipped him there and he shook his head and lumbered off defeated. But I've never found out how the wild ones do it, though I've no doubt they do, because of all those hollows I've told you about.

There are already some windfalls about - apples, pears, damsons and plums, and my word, aren't those wasps after the plums and greengages! Some of the apples are beginning to redden, the blackcurrants, gooseberries and vegetable marrows are all hard at it - and there are some spider's webs about, the first sign of Autumn, although you can already notice that the days are getting shorter - so summer's on the wane. Nearly all the field flowers are over, the feathery grasses are cut, some birds have already left us and others are silent while they prepare to go, but there is still plenty of colour about - blue hare-bells, tall golden rod, scarlet poppies, large ox-eyed daisies and all those plants with beautiful names down by and in the rivers and water-courses, the lilac wild mint, snow-white arrow-head, rose-tinted water-plantain, the pink flowers of knot-grass, purple loose-strife, dark-blue water violets, bog-pimpernel, common duck-weed, bur-weed, white water-lilies, the flower-bearing rushes, bladder-wort - oh yes, and of course where it grows there's the heather, and I've forgot one thing, red-coloured pheasant's eye, that has that other lovely name, rose-a-ruby - and then in the ditches there's cow-parsley, hemlock, charlock, sorrel, the bryonies - as well as all the caterpillars and slugs!

Gathering swallows twitter in the skies.

I said a while back about birds getting ready to go - and I meant the swallows as much as anything. They're beginning to congregate, and they form enormous communal roosts, often in beds of reed - and one of the most exciting sights I know is to see them all rise together just before dusk, and fly up in an almost vertical spiral, like leaves caught in a whirlwind. They go up and up, and then descend to their perches in the reeds, and sometimes there are so many of them that the reeds bend with the weight and some drown in the darkness.

You know there are less rats about in the country than there used to be, because you see, in the old days, when the corn was ricked, the rats made holes in the ricks, and stayed in them all the winter, breeding away quite undisturbed, because they literally lived in their own larder. And when a late rick was threshed in spring it was quite usual to have to kill several hundred rats and it was a legal requirement that the ricks were surrounded by rat-proof netting so they couldn't escape.

This morning I was half-way round Mr Woolley's estate before breakfast chasing after a tawny owl and before you get all upset about owls being on the Schedule of Protected Birds, and I shouldn't have been huntin' them, let me have my say. Because I wasn't really hunting him or wishing him any harm 'cos for nearly six weeks now, I've been rearing this owlet by hand. He was no more than a ball of fluff when some stranger called on me with him and said he'd found him abandoned by the old birds. That sort of thing often happens to me, you know. All sorts of folk who should know better, find young fledglings just out of the nest, and jump to the conclusion that they have been abandoned and will starve. And it's a lot of nonsense.

When young birds leave the nest they nearly always scatter and for quite a time the old birds go on feeding them exactly as they did when they were in the nest. As soon as the youngsters get hungry, they shout their heads off to be fed - and that's how the old birds find them.

So when anyone brings me a young fledgling, I tell them to take it back and put it down where they found it. The old birds'll look after it far better than the best foster-mother could.

The same applies to other young animals. Leverets - young hares - are the commonest I get brought because the old hare leaves them hidden in a form, or nest, of grass - because of course, they can't run very far or fast when they are tiny and are safer hidden than trying to escape. But busybodies who stumble across them, think they've been abandoned and try to rescue them.

But that young owl that was brought me was a different kettle of fish altogether. He was till downy and not nearly ready to fly, so I suppose some vandal had taken him out of the nest and he really would have starved if nobody had taken him in hand. So I reared him on meat, covered by fur or feathers to help his digestion, and now he can fly quite well. He has started to hunt a little for himself, but he's always come home for a bit of my easy grub by morning. Or he did until today.

So when he didn't report for cookhouse, I had a stroll round to see if I could see him - but no luck. He'll probably come back tonight when he's really hungry, or maybe he thinks he can fend for himself now - and I hope he's right, because Prue and I got to be real fond of him and we'll be missing him and wondering where he is and how he's getting on.

September

Harvest-home, harvest-home
We have ploughed, we have sowed,
We have reaped, we have mowed,
We have brought home every load,
Hip, Hip, Hip, harvest-home!

You might think that September was the end of the farmer's year but in fact it is also the month in which his year begins, for it all starts with ploughing, doesn't it? And nowadays farmers plough the stubble in at once - sometimes after burning it. And it can cause nasty accidents that, like nearly happened to young Tony Archer a year or two back when the wind changed suddenly and thick smoke came across the road he was driving along and he nearly went into the ditch.

It's a golden month is September. Corn harvest is over but the wild harvest begins. Ivy is in flower, and it's a favourite collecting point for bees who seem to be getting a bit weary now. There are still plenty of wasps, of course, but they'll decrease towards the end of the month when the first frosts come.

I was telling you about wasps and wasp-nests not long ago, but I've just remembered an old-fashioned way of catching them. You take two round glass garden cloches and put them one on top of the other, but you have to be careful that the lower one is damaged and has a hole at the top where the knob you lift it by was broken off. Then you perch the cloches on top of a couple of bricks, and you put some rotten fruit under the cloches between the bricks. This attracts the wasps and after they've eaten some they instinctively fly upwards. They spiral round inside the bottom cloche, then through the hole in the top, and get imprisoned in the space between the two. In my time I've seen such jars packed absolutely solid with wasps and hornets - but it's not as good as the old badgers I was telling you about destroying the wasp nests before they has time to grow - though of course, they also destroy them later on when they are as big as footballs as well!

Now, what was I on about? Oh yes, 'mellow fruitfulness'. It's the time for blackberries of course, they should always be eaten in September because by October, country folk say the devil has put his hoof on them and they're not safe - and there's commonsense in that like many folk tales because by then they're always infested by insects. Oh, and it's mushroom month!

I was telling you about them too - but I didn't tell you about 'horse-mushrooms' did I? Well, these are as big as dinner plates, and often weigh over a pound each, and they grow in the same spot year after year, and where that is is always a closely guarded secret. One of the worst country crimes is to *pick* a horse-mushroom, or common wild ones come to that. They must always be cut clean across the stems with a knife or the mycelium won't run underground and there will be no more of them. Good countrymen, who know where to look, go to great lengths to camouflage horse-mushrooms with bits of grass or leaves so they go on growing without being found by someone else. You see, in law, a mushroom is a wild fruit and can be picked by anyone without 'stealing'. Now one way of preventing this, is to plant a little domestic mushroom spawn nearby. It doesn't matter whether it grows or not, but you can put up a notice then saying 'Cultivated mushrooms' which it's illegal to pick, and so protect the big wild ones.

Have you noticed the sounds of September are different to other times of the year? In the woods, the leaves are beginning to loosen before falling, so the wind in them makes a dry brittle sound quite different from the rustle of the summer months. The tops of the trees, especially oaks, are literally swarming with flies too, so that on a quiet evening they sound like a distant aeroplane.

September evenings are still good for badger watching, except that you will be eaten alive by midges. The hazel-nuts are ripening but they say you shouldn't pick them before the leaves have a golden yellow tint which shows the nuts are ripe, but the grey squirrels will be flocking in from the farmlands to steal them before this.

Gordon Armstrong has got rid of as many of his resident squirrels as he can but he'll find a lot more on his hands from the invasion, and there's not much he can do about that except trying to catch some with Fenn traps, because you see, he won't want to disturb his game just before the season begins.

There are other wild fruits about of course, sloes on the blackthorn (whose leaves in the autumn are gold, crimson and purple, and from whose wood you can make handsome black walking-sticks and the Irishman's shillelagh) and crab-apples. Did you know that the crab-apple tree is the parent of all the cultivated apples we have?

The Michaelmas daisies, dahlias, and chrysanthemums are flowering, the out-of-door tomatoes ripening, daddy-long-legs are all over the place, the stars are shooting, the days are drawing in, and on still cold evenings, mists form in the hollows, sometimes only four or five feet high to begin with.

By morning the dew can be very heavy, and you can see it spangling the gossamer spider's webs. Some folk don't like them of course, but I like to see the big, fat garden spiders, striped like tigers, sitting in the middle of their big cartwheel webs. And when I went to have my bath last night, sitting in the bottom of it was the father-and-mother of all spiders.

Being a good countryman I picked her up carefully and popped her out of the window before I turned the tap on, because you see, all good countrymen think it will bring bad luck to kill a spider. Not that I'm very superstitious but it's just good sense not to harm spiders because they do so much good killing flies and other pests. And of course, they don't get into baths by climbing up the plug-hole as some think either, because below the plug-hole the pipe has a U-bend which always holds water to stop smells coming back up from the sewer, and spiders couldn't crawl through the water in that bend, so they drop into the bath off the ceiling and then can't climb out.

Everyone knows the story of Robert the Bruce's spider that kept try-try-trying again till he succeeded in climbing up the wall. Well, if there's a bit of wind or even a decent draught, they're much more efficient than that. They climb up whatever they can, a bit of twig or top of a wall - and just spin a web, and the web is so light that it floats off on the breeze till it touches something solid, often yards away, and the sticky bit of the web fastens to it, so all the spider has to do is to go across as neat as a walker on a tight-rope.

And that reminds me, there was a stranger in The Bull the other night who was on about spiders. This chap is technical manager in a factory which makes wire-ropes for cranes, and ships' hawsers, and that sort of thing, and he says the best engineer in the world can't hold a candle to the common spider. They can make up to seven different kinds of thread on what amounts to one machine, and even change the thickness as they go along! Now these threads are not all sticky because the spider wants to run along them, but the bits that catch the flies are. And the threads are three times as strong as steel-rope the same thickness - so a spider's web one inch thick if you could make one, could carry over seventy tons!

Do you know, I had a lovely surprise last week, quite like old times, it was. I went for a stroll down by the reed-bed, on the edge of the lake in the cool of the evening, when my eye was caught by what I took at first to be a bird's nest. It was about as big as a cricket ball, and quite as round, and it seemed to be lodged almost at the top of the reed stems. I thought it was the nest of a long-tailed tit, at first. Can-bottles we call them, because they weave a spherical nest, often in gorse, or something thick like that, and they line it with thousands of feathers. I was surprised that birds should be nesting so late in the year because most of them finished some time ago.

Wood pigeons, that make the woods cosy with their cooing, are among the few birds that still nest in autumn. They may make the laziest sound in nature, but they make up for it by their enthusiasm for breeding! Well, I had a closer look at the bird's nest I'd found in the reed-bed and it wasn't a bird-nest at all! It wasn't made of twigs, or bents of grass for one thing, but had been beautifully woven out of the leaves of the reeds so it was camouflaged exactly the same colour as its surroundings. The next thing I noticed was that it hadn't got an entrance hole, as a long-tailed tit's nest would have done, and the weave was so perfect that it held together tight enough to hold a nest of youngsters, but loose enough to let Mum shove *through the wall* of the nest to feed them.

I said the surprise was like old times. Well it was, except that the last nest I'd seen like it was in standing corn instead of a reed-bed. You see, it was the nest of harvest-mice. Whatever you think of ordinary mice, you wouldn't be human if you weren't charmed by a harvest-mouse. He's only a quarter as big as a house mouse, his coat is brilliant foxy-red and he can climb like a squirrel. They're called harvest-mice because of their love of nesting in standing corn, but modern farming methods, combine harvesters and not storing corn in ricks, has almost wiped them out.

In some parts of the country they've become very rare indeed, and I hadn't seen a nest for more than thirty years. But nature's marvellous. She lets species get very rare - but sees to it that very few get quite wiped out. So harvest-mice seem to have shifted their habitat from corn to reeds that have edible seeds - and which don't get chopped down by farm machinery! They live in wilder but safer cover now, and if you go blackberrying soon you may easily see one sharing the fruit with you!

You know, I reckons the second flowering of the rose is better than the first - they look much cooler and sweeter, and they lasts longer too. And there's the last of the butterflies now. 'Flowers on the wing' I've heard the Japanese call them. 'Flowers on the wing' - I like that, don't you?

We usually has our Flower and Produce Show fairly early in September and Carol Tregorran having her market garden and knowing all about it, usually organises it for us - and very well she does it too. And to my way of thinking, if it's the real spirit of the countryside you're after, then there's nothing to beat a village fruit, flower and vegetable show, even though it's always the wrong time of the year for some things - too late for the

sweat-peas, too early for the fattest dahlias, past time for the new potatoes, but right enough for the best half-dozen of brown eggs - and the time's always right for some sort of fruit-bottling, wine-making, and honey from the hive. As for Victoria Sponges, well - I've never been to a flower show yet at any time in the summer, when there wasn't Victoria Sponges sitting there with a judges' nibble out of each of them! And I knows my friends won't mind and won't think I'm biased if I say Doris's Victoria Sponges are always the best - and do you know why they won't mind? Because it's true, that's why!

Then there's all those runner beans, glossy big onions, matching marrows, trugs full of best all-round vegetable displays - and cauliflowers like those big white clouds you see in summer. Too bad that old Walter's best single rose was nowhere this year - you can't fool the judges by picking off a couple of rain-spotted outer petals! They know all right.

I had a bad night last night. Kept awake by coughin' I was. Ooh! not our Prue. She snores a bit but she hardly ever coughs. No, the row that disturbed me came from the meadow below our cottage window. A bunch of bullocks chose a patch so close to the wall to sleep on, that it sounded as if they was right under the bed. And they never stopped coughin' all night. Cattle often cough a lot at this time of year and country folk call it the hoost. And hoost's a fair description too.

It's really caused by a parasite that should have been got rid of with a dose from the vet - but lots of old farmers won't believe it. They say it's caused by spiders. There are always thousands of spiders in every field, but they're more obvious at this time of year as I said, because the morning dews are heavy now, and the webs show up. And true enough when I looked out of our bedroom window this morning, the grass was covered with a layer of shining spiders' webs. So it wouldn't be unreasonable to think that when the cattle grazed they'd sucked in the webs - which had made them cough. But it's really only coincidence that they get the hoost when the spiders' webs look thickest - and they should have had a dose as I said.

And there's another country belief about coughs that I'm not so sure about - though Dr Poole always laughs at it. In the Midlands, some of us call whooping-cough, chin-cough. Or some of us old 'uns do. It isn't very common now because modern drugs are too clever for it, but when I was a lad it was a horrid complaint, and I whooped on for weeks. Our doctor, he's been dead for years now, well, he couldn't make no headway with it and my mother got fed up with it, so she took me out at dawn into the fields and looked round till she found a big bramble bush. Now where the tip of a blackberry shoot touches the ground it often puts down suckers and roots itself, so that it's rooted at both ends in a solid loop. The old belief was that if you took a child at dawn and passed him three times under this loop, he'd be cured. But each time you put him under, you had to say 'Over briar, under briar, the child'll leave the chin-cough here'. Well she did all that, and she said it cured me all right, but when I told our doctor, he said it was more likely the cold morning air that did the trick! It was better than his physic, anyway, and I wish there'd been a handy briar to shove those cattle under last night I can tell you.

And I've got some more old country superstitions for you. Did you know that mushrooms won't grow any more, once someone has seen them? And that the clothes of the dead won't last long? And a very old one - that if a bridal party going to church meets a monk (that shows how old it is), a priest, a hare, a dog, cat, lizard or serpent, the marriage won't be happy! So you'd better be careful.

It's just as well it didn't mention moths because there are quite a lot of them about now - the spotted wood-leopard moth, the tiger-moth and the goat-moth among them.

Now, before we goes any further I expect you've been waiting for me to tell you about the name of the month as I have been doing. Well I am, and I'm not, if you follow me! By that I mean I'm going to deal with all the other months at once, and I can do that because at one time the year began in March, so September was the seventh month, October, the eighth, November, the ninth, and December the tenth, so now you see why I'm telling you about all of them at once!

I saw old Autumn in the misty morn
Stand shadowless, like Silence listening to silence.

You know, if there's one other thing as well as the swallows going as makes me feel as though the curtain's coming down on summertime as you might say, it's the last village cricket matches of the season being played.

Come harvest time in August, often the villages can't raise a side of a Saturday or a Sunday afternoon - they're all getting in corn while the sun shines. But come middle and late September cricket gets a final fling afore stumps is drawn after the last game of the season.

Mind you, I like to see a good football match as much as anybody but cricket on the green seems somehow more English to me, and watching it's a sight more comfortable, too! Maybe the excitement's not going on all the time like in football, except of course, when Penny Hassett plays Netherbourne. Deadly rivals they are. Going back to the Civil War, some says,

Penny Hassett being for the King, and Netherbourne for Cromwell. Anyroad it's always a real 'do or die' affair, and like as not I'll be over there.

When you're getting on in years a bit like I am, there are a number of ways of measuring the life you've had. Some go by successes, I suppose, or the number of jobs they've had, and others take a tally of their friends. Now my real friends, as opposed to acquaintances, can really be counted on the fingers of my hands. But the things I measure my life by are the dogs I've had, and that combines all three methods. Successes, jobs, and friends - all rolled into one! Because as a keeper dogs were my job. I couldn't work without them - and if they hadn't been successful, I wouldn't have had a job. And, of course, I've had plenty of friends among them too, as well as acquaintances. Some of the dogs which passed through my hands to be trained I used to grow too fond of, and it grieved me to part with them because I knew their masters wouldn't know enough about them to do them justice.

But the real dogs of my life, my own dogs, I could count on the fingers of one hand, because most of them lasted ten years or so, and I didn't get a youngster to follow on till the old dog was getting old enough to take it easy for a few years in retirement.

Those dogs - they were friends - real friends who gave me all they'd got, and never let me down. Most of them were very clever at their work too, so that folk who didn't know my name, sometimes described me as 'the keeper who has that marvellous dog'. And I was proud to bask in my dog's reflected glory I can tell you. I'm not much of a one for dog shows but I did have one old spaniel that won all before him in the show-ring - and I was that proud Prue had to tell me not to get swollen-headed!

Early this month over at Loxley they held what they called 'An Old Time Farming Festival' and I went to take a look at it. And I must say as I gave full marks to the organisers for the trouble they'd taken. They must've been working best part of the summer to get together all the stuff as was there, and beautifully planned it was too to give the crowds a good idea of what life on the farm was like around sixty or more years ago.

But what I think fetched the crowd most was a display of steam-ploughing, with a pair of twenty-ton old engines three hundred yards or so apart hauling a heavy five-furrow plough from one end of the field to the other with the wire hausers coiling around those great drums of theirs. There was power for you, with the fly-wheels spinning, and the stoker stoking, and the whistles screaming. Oh! and what a lovely smell of hot oil, and steam, and smoke, and the polished brass collars around their chimneys shining bright in the sunlight.

The Loxley farmer whose land it was all on was having his corn stubble ploughed deeper'n any tractor-drawn plough'd do it today. He'd left a couple of acres of long-straw wheat, and around three o'clock time, out comes as fine a pair of shire horses as ever I seen with the reaper and binder behind them. And to my mind there's no more handsome sight in farming than the muscles of a pair of big shires standing out, with the sails of the binder turning behind them and the corn sheaves neatly tied and ready for stooking to dry in the September sun.

There was hand-milking, and cream-skimming, and butter churning, - oh, and lots more to remind us old 'uns of other days and to show the youngsters something as they'd never seen before, and like as not would never see again. Of *course* things is quicker, and more efficient, and tidier these days, and I'm not one to go all dewy-eyed and nostalgic but - well, I enjoyed myself and, what's more, met a lot of old pals there - and had a pint or two with them.

When I was keepering, my Prue often didn't see much of me in this month because I was out in the woods from dawn to dusk, because you see pheasant shooting begins officially on

1 October - and woodcock too. Actually partridge shooting starts at the beginning of September but they've been getting much scarcer because of the stubble being ploughed up so quickly, the hedgerows having been grubbed up and the pesticides which have been used and which have poisoned so many of them. They have in fact, begun to increase again lately and there's a rare old argument going on between the keen shooters who want to get at them again and the conservationists who think they ought to go on the Schedule of Protected Birds.

You know there's a very special day for farming folk towards the end of the month - 29 September to be exact - it's the Day of St Michael and All Angels, or Michaelmas Day as it's usually known. It's a Quarter Day, we all know that, but for farmers it can be the day of change, for if a farmer decides to sell his farm, or buy a farm, or quit a farm if he's a tenant, and maybe move somewhere else, then it's generally come Michaelmas that the deed must be done, as you might say. And incidentally 29 September is 'new' Michaelmas Day. 'Old' Michaelmas used to be on 11 October, which is why geese are not really ready now by Michaelmas, but even so they taste much better then to my mind than they do if left till Christmas which is the modern fashion.

The swallows are making them ready to fly,
Wheeling out on a windy sky,
Goodbye summer, goodbye, goodbye.

Many of the migratory birds have gone by now, but the swallows are still forming up on the telephone wires and congregating in vast flocks to roost at nights. They're ready for their flight to Africa now and haven't they been making a song about it! Just as it gets light in the mornin' they wake us up with a sweet melody that I never associate with swallows - until I hear it! And they're such wonderful flyers and they're lovely to look at, with their blue-black glossy plumage and chestnut fronts. They're the nicest type of do-gooders too with all the flies they kill - and on top of all that as I said, they sing as sweet as a throstle.

But they have a lot to put up with some summers. For a start, sometimes the mud isn't gooey enough for them to build their nests easily. I watched a pair in the old pigsty once, and they had to go right down to the edge of the lake for each beakful of mud and when they got back more than half of it crumbled and fell on the floor. I got so sorry for them I collected some good clay and made mud-pies in a bucket and put it by the water's edge where the birds were collecting that poor stuff from and they soon cottoned on to the fact that mine was top quality stuff from their own builders' merchant and left all the sandy stuff, and took mine, and it worked like a charm. Within forty-eight hours the nest was done and they were in the egg-laying business! But when they did get their eggs laid and chicks hatched, their troubles were only just beginning. The first brood did quite well and four strong chicks eventually flew away but a few weeks later when the next family was getting toward the launching stage, I noticed they seemed uncommonly keen to quit the nest. I thought it was four-to-a-bed in a hot summer, and I didn't blame them. Just a bit of overcrowding, I thought. But it wasn't that because when they did fledge, they hit the deck and couldn't fly properly. I picked them up to see what the matter was - and they were absolutely lousy. Simply covered from head to foot in mites. Bloodsucking mites, which had made them too weak to fly. I was too late to save them but I sprayed the nest with an insecticide and the old birds were successful with the third brood. Now they're ready to go, and I shall be real sorry to lose them. They're really gathering, hundreds of them on the telephone wires, twittering, and preening themselves, playing catch-me-if-you-can with their new-flown youngsters and will soon all be gone.

You know, I really belive I once saw the last swallow of summer! I was over Norfolk way early October time, looking out over a sea as still as a mill-pond. And there, heading south, just over the waves, was six swallows, and five minutes later four more. Then just a pair, and way, way behind one all on his own. Do you know I felt quite a lump in my throat? The last swallow of the year - and the end of summer.

Now you may not believe this story, but I'm not having you on - I read it in a letter in a paper the other day. It seems as though there was this keen bird-watcher, a Spaniard living way up in the north of his country. It was September a year ago when he caught a swallow and ringed it. And just by way of a shot-in-the-dark as you might say, he tucked a little note under the ring on the bird's leg, saying - in Spanish, of course - 'I wonder where you spend the winter?'

Well, blow me if this last spring the bird didn't come back to its old nest in a barn at the back of his house. And there was a little bit of paper still under the ring. Ah, but it was a different bit of paper, and it said - in Spanish again - 'I spend my winters back of a grocery store, Teneriffe, Canary Islands.' Would you believe it - that little swallow had come into the hands of another bird lover all those miles away! Chap with a good sense of humour, too! Nice, isn't it?

But the days are drawing in, aren't they? And there's quite a nip in the air sometimes so Prue and I puts on a fire as soon as we gets in of an evening and now I'm getting on a bit I draws up to it and I'm quite glad I hasn't to be out and about at all hours like I used to be - makes me think of that last swallow sometimes, it does.

October

Onion skins very thin
A mild winter is coming in:
Onion skins thick and tough
Coming winter cold and rough.

I was having my usual dinner-time drink in The Bull last Monday with Dan, when a pal of mine from Netherbourne who I hadn't seen for a month or two came in. 'Morning, Tom,' he says, 'another Snobs Day come round, and it don't seem a week since the last.' 'Why, Sam,' says I, 'it's years since I heard anyone talk about Mondays being Snobs Day. Meks me think of old times.'

Now don't ask me why at one time all village bootmakers and cobblers was known as 'snobs', or 'snobbys'. They just were, and Mondays was always the day as they took off, for most of them was at their busiest Saturdays and Sundays repairing workaday boots for them as had to be out and about on the farms and that, Monday mornings.

And I'd be a liar if I was to say as most snobbys didn't make quite a day of it Mondays, behind their pint pots in the pubs, and I'm not blaming them. Of course, one time we had our own snobby in Ambridge, chap name of Harris, though nobody ever did know his first name. He was just Snobby Harris, and that was that.

Cheerful old chap, Snobby Harris, always smiling, and I can see him now sitting at his bench in the front room of his cottage which was his workshop. Mouthful of nails as like as not, but he managed to give you a grin through them. He was a little fellow, and the skin of his hands and face was smooth as an old billiard ball as if it had been pickled in cobblers' wax, as I daresay it had over the years.

Never rode a bicycle, did Snobby, he'd walk the lanes for miles delivering boots to folks as lived far out of the village. Of a night-time you could see Snobby's little hurricane lamp as he always carried, bobbing along the Penny Hassett road on his way home. He always said as walking was the only way to enjoy the countryside, and he always had something he'd picked up on his travels - mushrooms, maybe, a fistful of wild garlic, some sweet chestnuts or a half-dozen crab-apples. And he'd always offer you something.

Monday really was Snobby Harris's day, and in The Bull of an evening, and sometimes of a dinner-time, he'd play his old brown fiddle and sing old songs - not all of 'em for the ears of the ladies neither I can tell you! But him and his like aren't around any more I'm sorry to say.

You know, if somebody told me I could only go into the country for one day in the year, I think I'd choose October. The colours are wonderful, shades of gold, and yellow, and brown in the leaves matching the fresh-cut stubble and the new-ploughed soil. And to me the skies are never clearer or bluer than in October on a good day.

Of course, it's a time of slow decay too, the leaves are starting to fall, you begin to get glimpses of views which have been hidden for months by the trees, and there's that *smell* of Autumn. The cherry trees are scarlet and there are some apples left but the nights are often cold and damp, though the Hunter's Moon can look wonderful on a clear night, can't it? And when we get a spell of good weather towards the middle of the month, as we often do, it's called St Luke's Little Summer or, of course, others call it an Indian Summer - and that has nothing to do with India as you might think, but it was called that in the last century because the Indians in North America used to store crops and prepare for the winter during their fine spell in the autumn. The weather men say our kind is caused by the North Atlantic anticyclone spreading to the north-east, but whatever causes it, it can be very beautiful, can't it? And it brings out the butterflies - painted-ladies, tortoise-shells, and red admirals - which were just going to settle down to hibernate. And it's the time for Michaelmas daisies, and those always attract butterflies and bumble bees.

And October is a fine time for birdsong too because most of them have got over the moult, which is a very lowering, uncomfortable, and miserable business for them, so they sing away for joy I think, though the boffins say they are really staking their claim to the territory they hope to occupy next season! The robin, the wren and the lark are among the best songsters just now - and the birds are not only in good voice but in fine feather too!

Most of our summer migrants have gone or are just about to go, but what so many people forget is the birds who *come* to us for the winter, fieldfares, redwings, and snipe from Scandinavia, barnacle geese from Spitzbergen, white-fronted geese from Siberia and pink-footed ones from Iceland, and wood-pigeons and starlings from the Continent to boost the local population, they all come to spend their winter with us.

Migration is a very mysterious business of course. There are two main reasons for it, to feed and to breed, but that doesn't explain why the arctic tern should fly 11,000 miles from us every year to spend the winter in the Antarctic, or why the painted-lady butterfly should leave Africa and come all the way to stay with us when they couldn't possibly survive the winter here, does it?

It seems it may be chemical changes in the body brought about by the length of the day that makes them do it, and they start to get ready for the journey by eating more and putting on weight to keep them going. Of course, salmon migrate too, coming back every year from the sea to breed in the rivers where they were born, whereas eels do it the other way round, living in freshwater rivers and taking off for the Sargasso Sea to breed - rum thing nature, isn't it?

The autumn winds soon bring the leaves tumbling off, the walnut usually sheds hers first, then the ash, and often the oak is the last of all, but the wind brings the acorns pattering down first. And deer and pheasants will go a long way to feed on them, but if the acorn crop is too big there is a danger that cattle will eat too many of them and get poisoned. In the old times when villagers had common rights in woods, pigs were put in to eat the acorns, partly because it helps to make good and cheap bacon, but also so the cattle didn't get too many. Even deer can get acorn poisoning some years, and I did hear tell there were some casualties in the London parks a while back. Deer and cattle love chestnuts too, and deer and sheep like ivy, though some people think it is poisonous. I expect you know the old song 'Hares-eat-oats and mares-eat-oats, but little lambs-eat-ivy!'

I was talking a while back of the beauty of autumn but I thinks, whatever the season, the real beauty of our countryside depends on trees. I don't mean blankets of pine trees stretching out into forests, I mean our native English trees. Oaks and beech, elm and ash, hawthorn and holly.

And if you think about it, it was gamekeepers like I used to be - or our employers - who were responsible. You see in my opinion, the best scenery of all is rolling parkland with small woods, coppices and spinneys dotted about all over it. You get all the blending colours and shapes you don't expect there, which look as if England has always been like that. But it hasn't. Some of it was laid out by the great landscape gardeners like Capability Brown - and even more was designed by the shooting and hunting men so that pleasants could be flushed from one wood to fly over the guns to the next, or so that hounds would find a fox there. But whatever the purpose, whether scenery was deliberately planned by artists, or was a practical pattern laid out by sportsmen - it's the trees that make it. Trees with all the greens of spring and the tints of autumn. Trees which still look lovely in winter with no leaves because it's only then that you can see their real shape which has been hidden all the summer.

But there's another thing beside trees that goes to make the pattern of our countryside - and that's the hedgerows, or it used to be. I went up on the hill above Arkwright Hall for a stroll the other evening, and it struck me then that the cleverest artist could never have dreamed up a picture half as beautiful as what lay stretched out at my feet right along the vale. No planners had got at it with their rulers and compasses, and it had never been divided into neat strips so that everyone could have a fair share. If they did the same job of parcelling up the English countryside now, I expect it'd look no better than the dog's breakfast they make of these New Towns, as neat and

regular as spiders' webs but not half so interesting. You see the way the countryside at my feet had been laid out seemed to have more to do with that rolling English drunkard who traced the original rolling English roads. Now these roads, they're really no more than lanes round us, these roads are bordered by the hedges that trace the whole pattern. The scientists say you can tell how old they are by the number of species of trees and bushes growing in them. The more species, the older the hedge, though I can't help thinkin' that a good many of the old landowners, who employed chaps like Capability Brown to lay out their estates, probably planted a variety to make them look attractive in their own time.

Anyroad, the hedges below where I was were mostly blackthorn and quickthorn. The leaves had dropped early and in the drier patches the quickthorn, that's the hawthorn, was as ruddy with berries as a weather-beaten cheek. And the blackthorns that were covered in white flowers before the leaves came in spring, had got sloe berries as black as black. So I wandered down the hill and came home along the lane-side hedge which traced the old parish boundary. Now what I was really doing was to have a look for some likely walking-stick rods as I did when I was a lad, which I told you about.

Blackthorn makes wonderful thumb-sticks and if you get the blacksmith to put a blade like a little hoe on the end, you can 'spud out' thistles as you go round! But I also picked a pound of sloes, which have a bloom better than the grapes people take to hospitals, and I shall get Prue to prick them, add a pound of sugar, and a bottle of gin, because we think Christmas is never complete without a glass of sloe-gin.

Early in the month I went over to Loxley where an old pal of mine had decided to call it a day - he'd been a tenant farmer there for close on forty years and it suited him when it was time to go. And there in the big meadow, back of the two big barns and the farmyard, was all my old pal's lifetime come under the auctioneer's hammer. His ploughs and harrows, his tractors and cultivators, his horse-hames and potato-riddles, his scythes and bean-hooks, and his feeding-troughs and hen-houses - all the gear, new and old, as goes to make up the working life of a farm. There was even a pair of old two-tined hay-forks and a leather belt what had been used to turn the threshing-tackle with the old steam-engine.

I bought in a wooden hay-rake and one of the hay-forks just for sentiment's sake. Oh, but it's sad to see a farm sale, all of a man's life, some of it a lot of rusty old iron, some of it shining new and full of hope, laid out there under the chestnut leaves for everyone to look at.

But round about the same time early in the month, we had our Harvest Thanksgiving, and what a sight it was in our church with a great arrangement of the flowers of the season in the middle of the altar - fat dahlias and chrysanths, Michaelmas daisies and, of course, beech-leaves just turning. And all beautifuly arranged by Doris and Laura, and the other ladies. Why, the very moment you went in you could smell all the good things of the land - the scent of the rosy apples lined up on the window-sills, the hop-vines with their dried cones of fruit hung in garlands round the pulpit, and the corn-sheaves under the chancel-arch. Then the harvest loaf - there's always got to be a big home-baked harvest loaf, shining as if it had been varnished, and this year a crusty little harvest-mouse sitting on the side of it, specially baked by Martha Woodford.

Yes, thanks be for the harvest, not only for the corn, and the spuds, and the fruit, but all the preserves as the ladies of the village made - with everything going, as usual, to the old folks' home in Borchester. And how we sang those traditional old harvest hymns like 'We plough the fields and scatter' and 'All is safely gathered in' - it's the sort of thing that brings the whole village together into one big family.

Do you know what a bothy is? Well, if you have a look in the walled garden of most stately homes, you'll see a row of what look like single-roomed cottages. One-up, one-down, if they was lucky, but usually single-rooms and those are bothies. They were built for the single gardeners, house-boys and stable-lads, who slept there and usually ate in the kitchen of the Big House. They were the lads who mucked the stables out, cleaned the dog-kennels, weeded the borders, and all the other odd jobs you could get done when labour was cheap. I found it a wonderful apprenticeship myself, but modern lads might jib at it I suppose. Times change, don't they?

And talking of how times have changed one of the most cunning poachers I ever had to deal with went by the name of the Whippet. He was a wiry little feller who looked as if his ribs would stick through his shirt if the wind blew in the right direction. Heaven knows he poached enough game off us, but I think he must have sold it all, for he just couldn't have been that thin if he'd eaten it! So his nickname wasn't really very original. He did look as thin as a whippet. And oddly enough he kept a whippet too. Not one of these modern silk-coated show dogs mind, that look as if their legs would break if they tried to trot, but Whippet's whippet must have had a bit of a cross in him. I should think 'is mother had been frightened by a sheep-dog because he was rough-coated and strong, although he could run fast enough to catch a hare. I used to wonder if Whippet had bought a running dog because he looked like one, or if he'd grown to look like his dog after he'd kept one for a bit, as some folk say happens. Until last week I'd got an open mind about it, but I happened to have an hour to kill in Borchester one day, while Prue was in the hairdresser's, and I saw a notice saying Dog Show. I stood on the steps wondering if it was worth the entrance money when I noticed a lot of exotic breeds going in that I really know nothing about, so my curiosity was aroused. When I got inside my eyes stood out on stalks. It could have been coincidence I know, but the first show-ring I came to was for the dachshunds, and I don't believe there was an owner above five foot high - and it might have been my imagination or pure coincidence, but they all looked snipey nosed! And you know, those dachshunds reminded me of an old crossbred bull-terrier I had as a kid. Not that he was like a dachshund, of course, quite the reverse. He was thick set, with a bullet-head and a strong jaw, but my pals all said I looked just like him. Then I thought of old Whippet, the poacher, who looked like his dog, and I forgot all the exotic breeds I'd come in to look at. I wandered round instead looking at any old dog and the chap or woman who was showing him in the ring. And do you know, I think there's something in it! The winner in the class for setters and pointers was such a good-looking woman I wondered which end of the lead the judge had looked at. And I swear the man with the winning bull-dog looked exactly like Winston Churchill. You just put the theory to the test with any of your pals who own dogs, and you'll find it's not as far fetched as you might think.

I see last week as the travelling folks have come back to the village with a couple of cars and a couple of caravans, parked at the back of Tony Archer's Willow Farm. The same lot's been coming back twice a year to Ambridge for all of ten years I'd say. First it's for the pea-picking and now of course, it's for the potatoes.

Now there's travelling folk, and there's travelling folk, and it's the worst of them as gets the best of them a bad name, and I reckon as our lot's among the best. Mind you, I used to keep an eye on them where my birds was concerned! And if 'it's their delight to go poaching on a shiny night' as the old song goes, then I never caught one of them at it. And they keeps themselves to themselves, and *work*... you never see the like, the way they scuttles down the rows in the potato fields and fill up the boxes - leaves the Ambridge ladies nowhere. I reckon as most villages has what you might call their 'hard core' of potato-lifting ladies, and a bright sight they makes strung out over the fields on a fine October day in working slacks, blouses, and head-scarves all the colours of the rainbow. The village ladies always seems to get on well together, as if it was a party, but there's a difference between the village folk and the travelling-folk - there's nothing of the party about it for them, they're in it for the money, hard work, hard cash, and then away. And our lot - why, you'd never know as they'd been there, they leaves things so clean and tidy. Sometimes I almost envies them the life on the open road. Every man's hand's against them some folks say. Well, I reckon there's one hand they manages to escape anyroad - and that's the tax inspector's!

At the bottom end of September, pheasants always used to fill my mind. You see a keeper's job is to provide sport for the guvnor, and you couldn't dream up harder material to work on than pheasants. Like women, the more beautiful they are, the more stupid they seem to get! If there's a cattle drinking trough they can fall into when they're young, you may be sure some of them will drown there. And they'll walk round the end of a row of wire-netting, and peep, and cheep trying to get back through it, till a two or four-legged poacher hears them - or the keeper rescues them.

I've had a marvellous life and made some grand friends in the profession, so that making the final break with keepering was more than a milestone to me, though Prue and I have settled down well at the Garden Centre now, even if we did have trouble with those rhododendrons a while back.

It'll be full moon before long and I reckon the week of the full moon that comes in October is often the most beautiful in the whole year. I don't mean just autumn colours, golds, and reds, and yellows all merging together, and I don't mean the beautiful smell of new-ploughed soil when the harvest stubbles have been buried and sown with next year's crop. What fills my eyes with delight is a sight that very few people see. The countryside at night. Moonlight in woodland is soft enough to take the harsher colours until they all merge into delicate silvery tints. And you haven't appreciated the real beauty of trees until you've seen them silhouetted against the moonlight white of scudding clouds.

One of the snags about being a gamekeeper - and one of the joys too - was that we worked such odd hours and we were out at night as often as in the day-time, keeping an eye on the young pheasants we'd reared, and I used to enjoy the eerie calls of the owls, and the tiny rustles of mice and voles that get lost in daylight sounds. It wasn't all airy-fairy though! Just as you're getting poetic about soft winds whispering through golden leaves you could be startled out of your wits by a gun going off almost in your shadow. Some poaching rogue who was more enchanted by the solid black of a roosting cock pheasant than all the picturesque stuff that made the old masters' pictures famous, it'd be.

Old-fashioned poachers like Joe Grundy are as rare now as horses pulling ploughs though. Most of them have been replaced by sneak thieves with rifles in cars taking pot-shots from the roadside. Mind you, I used to have quite a soft spot for some of the old rogues but the modern ones - never!

Seeing Prue collecting hazelnuts the other day reminded me of an old country superstition that I heard when I was a boy, and that was that a girl should put three nuts on the bars of a grate naming two of them after herself and her lover. When one cracks or jumps, it means her lover will be unfaithful, if one begins to blaze or burn, he loves her, but if the one she's named after them both burn together they will be married. I reckon a lot of nuts used to get used up this way in the old days!

Oh, and did you know that if a grave is opened on Sunday there'll be another dug in the week?

We don't do it so much in the south of course, but 31 October is Hallowe'en, and in northern counties of England it's known as Nutcrack Night, and there's a great crunching of nuts and ducking in water for apples - and do you remember, those turnips we used to scoop the inside out of and dig holes for the eyes and mouth and put a candle in? All too busy watching the telly now I suppose, for things like that.

Have you got your fruit tree catalogues yet? You should have by now, you know - and get your bulbs planted, and your digging and manuring done if you can. But there are a lot of pests about, aren't there? Wireworm, clickbeetle, woodlice and centipedes to name just a few. Still you ought to be getting some good celery, leeks, and parsnips now so you can have some tasty soups and casseroles to keep the cold out.

I've just been down to the lake by Arkwright Hall - I always enjoys it there at this time of the year. The ducks are in full, gaudy plumage, and gathering together in winter flocks again

after going off in pairs all the summer to breed. And flocks of geese have flown in to join them and the noise down there at dawn and dusk is better than the finest orchestra. But it's not just an orchestra of big sounds. The curlews are back from the estuaries and the continent, as well as from nesting grounds on the moorlands. And no cry I know can touch a curlew's for wildness and purity. The winter woodcock are coming in too and settling in the woods. Mr Woolley and his shooting pals love them because they can dodge, and weave, and twist, and turn, so they're about the hardest bird to hit. They sort the men out from the boys all right they do.

Last night I woke to hear my first buck call of the season. They're fallow deer in our park, with a wonderful spread of antlers flattened, or palmated, at the ends. And for most of the year they're silent unless anyone startles them, when they sometimes 'bark' with a loud staccato noise. But at this time of year towards the bottom end of October, they come into mating condition and each buck chooses his rutting-stand. He thrashes the trees with his antlers, often doing a tremendous amount of damage in a sort of ritual build-up of temper to put himself in fighting mood to see-off any rival bold enough to challenge him. And between these displays of temper he groans, and that's what I heard the other night. It isn't really a groan, of course, it's a challenge. If you didn't know what it was, you might think it a symptom of very bad indigestion because it sounds more like a throaty belch than a threat.

But I always love to hear the deer calling, because to me it's the spirit of autumn. I don't need to alter my clock to tell me summer time has finished because I know it has when the first buck calls.

Depending a bit on the weather the fallow rut can be very short, just a matter of a few days. He selects the area where he's going to make his stand to warn off any rivals; he makes scrapes with his fore-feet, sort of hollows in the mud a yard or so across; he shadow-boxes any saplings in sight, and he groans! This isn't just a warning to rivals. It's an invitation to the does which collect round him as a kind of faithful harem - until a better buck arrives!

And talking of warnings, here's one for you. Wild fallow deer are very shy and will run away if they see you. But deer in public parks sometimes lose their fear of man, and the males are very dangerous in the rut. They are quite as bad as a savage bull, so don't you hang around if a buck seems menacing!

Now after the rut, when the old bucks are spent, the young ones take over, but the row they make diminishes. Next week will about see the end of it, and the herd will split up again. The does will go off to feed and gossip a bit I suppose, about the merits of the swains who picked them up in nature's own Paul Jones, and the bucks will quieten down.

To my way of thinking, especially in a country village like Ambridge, it's the slow changing of the seasons that makes for the variety that's really the spice of life. The village is a very different place in October from what it's like in the height of summer. Oh, there may be more going on in the summertime - sometimes almost too much, what with fêtes, and cricket matches, flower-shows, gymkhanas, coach-outings, Carnival Queens and all that. And there's cars and strangers everywhere. But now - well, we can all settle back and be our real selves again. The rhythm of life gets more into order as the curly brown chestnut leaves fall, and Sid and Polly's chairs in the garden of The Bull gets taken indoors, and the first frosts cut down the dahlias, and there's a big bright fire to welcome you of an evening, and the curtains are drawn to make everything peaceful and cosy. There are the kids throwing sticks to fetch down the conkers, the nuts in the hedgerows, the hips and haws, the sloes and spindleberries round the lanesides, and the smoke from cottage chimneys going straight up in the air around tea-time of a quiet day - beautiful, it is!

November

Frost in November to hold a duck
There follows a winter of slush and muck.

Mind you I don't agree with that one myself, but the first frosts in the month will kill off the last of the mushrooms and make the last blackberries go mushy - though as I told you some countryfolk don't eat blackberries after the end of September. And although we always think of November as a foggy month, February is usually worse - though mind you, this month is often pretty gloomy, with rain, wind, dull grey skies, decaying leaves and that tangy smell you get from them when they're wet. It's a great month for bonfires, of course, and not only on Guy Fawkes Day. Did you know that heather burning is legal in England from the first of the month to 31 March? Now that's not as useless a bit of information as you might think, because any bit of high ground that has heather on it could hold a few sheep, and the only way to improve it for them is to burn off the old plants.

You should be pruning your new fruit trees and your new roses now but there's still brussels sprouts, purple sprouting broccoli, celery and leeks going, and perhaps a few straggly chrysanthemums. And there's still colour in some of the berries besides holly, things like sloes, bullaces, cranberries, the berries on 'Butchers' Broom which can be as large as a cherry, and the deep purple of wild cornel or dogwood berries. Of course, by now you can see the bony skeletons of the trees - and beautiful they can look too, outlined against the sky.

Not many folks has a good word to say for November but I'm not one of them. We'd a rare old gale just afore the start of the month and it fetched the leaves down in showers - from the elms, the ash and of course the beech. But a useful one it was too, for plenty of dead wood was fetched down into the bargain, and the Vicar said something as I shan't forget in a hurry - 'Old Mother Nature's busy with her pruning hook today, Tom,' he said. And that's just about the truth of it!

Of course, the oak-leaves is about the last to drop, and they're a pretty sight early in the month, all ginger-looking with the bare branches of the other trees around them. But I do admit I do once in a way agree with the folk who haven't a good word to say for the month, it can sometimes seem neither one thing nor another, all the best of autumn done with and the hard bit of winter still to come, that is if we gets a really hard bit. We'll just have to wait and see, won't we?

I was at John Tregorran's place a week or two back and a proper old November day it was - with a sky like a wet saucepan lid, the trees dripping with damp, and the last leaves falling off. Depressing sort of day, and I said as much to John. And he showed me a poem that some chap had written about November. Now let's see if I can remember some of it - ah, yes, this is how it goes:

No sun - no moon,
No morn - no noon...
No shade, no shine, no butterflies, no bees,
No fruits, no flowers, no leaves, no birds,
November!

Sort of the last word of the month as you might say! Not that he was right about the no birds bit. There's a lot of birds - take the lapwings for a start, big crowds of them settling to feed on the ploughland with those cocky little crests of theirs; and starlings at sunset time, thousands of them wheeling in the sky as if they was a single bird - there's a sight I never tires of. And all the little finches getting together for winter company and feeding in the hedgerows. And as for the wood pigeons over here from the continent - they'll attack kale, clover root, and any market garden greens that are going - and it's much harder to get your casual sportsman to come and shoot them than it used to be because of the price of cartridges now - wicked it is.

And there's usually a lot of migrating woodcock about. A few stay to breed here in the summer but their camouflage is so good that your only chance of finding a nest, except by stumbling across it accidentally, is to spot the sitting bird's bright eyes - eyes which being set on the sides of its head give it all-round vision. When you come on her, she may sit tight, or if she has young, she may fly off. Mind you there is a great deal of argument about whether she carries her young off to safety or not. Some say she picks them up between her legs and carries them off, while others say the young get entangled in her feathers and are carried off by accident.

Shooting men love woodcock because they get up unexpectedly and have a kind of twisting flight, so that they are 'sporting' quarry. If you get a reliable witness to confirm that you shot a-right-and-a-left, that is one with each barrel, a top wine merchant, it's said, will give you a bottle, or is it a case? of sherry.

But a bird as we've been short of these past few years is jays, don't ask me why. But one morning last week I saw a couple of them and I thought to myself what handsome birds you are with your rosy backs and them blue-and-white chequerboard wings of yours. Now we all knows as the jay is no friend to the gamekeeper but for all that I was happy to see the pair of them because - well, they are so beautiful. And you know, even if I'd had my gun with me I wouldn't have found it in my heart to shoot them!

And this set me thinking what really handsome creatures so many of the beasts and birds are, as we call 'pests', and though we got to control them, I always has a bit of a qualm as I cocks my gun and lets fly at something as pretty as a grey squirrel - and real pests they are when there's eggs or young birds in the nest.

Then take magpies - they're another fine-looking bird with their long tails and black-and-white plumage. Regular jokers too, in their way, like jackdaws, though there's not much of the pest about the old 'daw'. One time of day many a countryman had a pet jackdaw perched on his shoulder but that's a thing as you don't see much these days.

Stoats, now - they're handsome beasts with their chestnut coats, and weasels, like little gingery pencils streaking across a lane. Shrews apart, I reckon as the weasel's about the most savage and brave creature for its size in the country. Oh, and I near forgot the wild cat, though we're not exactly bothered with them around Ambridge!

It doesn't seem so very long ago since we was all thrilled to see the first collared doves as had come into the country from the Middle East by way of Western Europe - 1952 or 1953 it was. Pretty birds they are, but now they're a regular pest, especially among folks as keeps chickens. And the poor old bullfinch, he's another on the 'unwanted list'. Talk to any fruit farmer about bullfinches and he'll have a short answer to that one! But what a fine chap he is, the cock bullfinch, with his cherry chest and white rump. It's a fact you see, pest or no, the Lord never created anything that isn't good-looking in its own way.

You know there's any amount of 'needle' in the country between the genuine countryfolk and the outsiders - those who outbid them for country cottages and in sport - and now the shooting season is with us again, I wants to talk about the 'shooters' and the 'sportsmen'. Of course, I knows there are many folk who disapproves of both, but there it is, I've been a gamekeeper all my life so you can hardly expect me to agree with you there, can you? Now, the pheasant shooting season begins legally in October but the reared birds are not very wild nor strong on the wing till November. So sportsmen only shoot lightly round their boundaries early in the season to drive straying birds back onto the shoot and to teach them to be gun-shy - and therefore more difficult, or sporting, to shoot.

'Shooters' on the other hand, - spiv syndicates, usually from faraway towns - are only interested in getting a return for their outlay and don't worry about giving their quarry a sporting chance. Anything that moves is fair game to them and they try to squeeze the very last pheasant out of it - and they are not popular with the genuine locals.

Now the other country sport about which there's so much controversy is hunting - and I'm not going to risk my neck by going into the pros and cons of it here, though there's no denying it's very much a part of country life and a great many people do it, though you'll remember Jill Archer was dead against it when young Shula went. Anyroad, although cubbing started as soon as the corn was cut in late August or September, it was only to 'enter' young hounds, and teach 'em that however wrong it is to kill cats, foxes are all right. Well, the real season often starts with a 'lawn meet' at some rich man's house, or the house of someone who'd like to be thought rich, and before the hounds move off stirrup cups are provided - and they are only provided for those in hunting pink - which is really red, and may only be worn by full members of the hunt and not by subscribers. Now, some of the people who have lawn meets don't know this, and dole out bad sherry to anyone on top of a horse, instead of good port and whisky to those who should be getting it - snobbish it may be but I likes some of these old traditions to be respected myself.

Now I reckon you'll be surprised to hear I went hunting with hounds the other day - and it wasn't a fox we were after it was a human being! You see I was invited to have a day with a pack of *bloodhounds* and as it is about the only country sport I'd never tried, I was delighted to have a go. They look very fearsome too, I can tell you. Bloodshot eyes and slobbering jowls, with voices as deep as church bells. But that's all window-dressing. They're really very sloppy and affectionate, so that if they do catch their quarry, he gets nothing worse than a wet face, where they lick at him.

The hunt begins with a good runner - and he's got to be good! - setting off to lay a trail about five miles long. And because he can choose where he goes, he avoids seed-corn, or pheasant coverts, or market garden crops, so the followers don't go where they're not welcome. But before he starts, he leaves his jacket so the huntsman can let his hounds get a scent of the quarry. The one thing they have to be careful about is that the quarry runs in leather boots, as rubber wellies don't transmit human scent very well.

Our huntsman gave the quarry about three quarters of an hour's start, then he let his hounds out of the van, showed 'em the jacket - and blew his hunting horn. You never heard such a shindig. They made a foxhound sound like a choirboy with laryngitis, and they sounded fierce enough to eat him. It made the hairs bristle up the nape of my neck, and I wondered if they really were as gentle as they're suposed to be!

The fascinating thing was that I'd seen exactly where the quarry had run, and the hounds were anything up to a couple of hundred yards down-wind of his line, but although his scent had drifted, it still clung to bushes and grass down-wind strong enough for their delicate noses to follow. And I learned more about scent in an hour than you could pick up in a lifetime seeing ordinary dogs work.

Now I expect as most of you who've got a bit of garden have it all dug over by now, and everything looking nice and tidy, and spick and span for the spring - all the spring bulbs in, and the wallflowers, and the forget-me-nots, and those polyanthus plants which was dug in for summer in a nice damp corner. I daresay you've got them split up, and bedded out by now. Leastways, I hope so for your sakes. For to my way of thinking there's few things more depressing in a flower-garden than to see it still in a right old tangle come mid-November, and not cleaned up, and gone up in bonfire smoke, which is the cleanest and sweetest smell of all on an autumn day to my mind.

Not that I'm sitting back, smug as you please, and saying: 'We got ours done, and what about you?' It's just that when it's done, what better feeling is there than to clean and oil most of your garden tools, cut the grass for the last time, and then say: 'Aaah, now I can sit back and take it easy till the spring.'

Of course, the flower-garden's woman's work - among most countryfolk, that is. Most of us chaps like to eat what we grows. Though, I always gives my Prue a hand when it comes to the autumn digging and that, and like as not I'll do the wrong thing. 'Oh, Tom,' she'll call out, 'just look what you've done in that corner - dug up all the little whatevers as I've been nursing since the springtime. Oh, Tom...!' You can't win with a woman in her flower-garden, any more'n you can tell her as getting stuck into the garden catalogues middle of November's not the best of times. 'I'll tell you what I'll have next spring, Tom,' she said the other night, 'old-fashioned auriculas - look - here - lovely, aren't they...?' Oh dear, what's the use of telling her as there's not a square inch of garden to put them in after all the other spring things we put in already - even if we can get them a bit cheap now we're running Mr Woolley's Garden Centre for him.

Just about now the hedgehogs, and dormice, and bats will be going into hibernation, and when this happens they practically go into a state of suspended animation and their respiration slows down to one breath about every five minutes! And provided they don't actually freeze, the lower the temperature of their bodies the better, because when everything slows down like this they use very little energy and have very little to excrete - actually the ideal temperature is about 6 degrees centigrade - but of course you'll remember I told you a bit about hibernation before.

A lot of farmers will be mating their sheep now, and will have 'raddled' the ram. In the old days they rubbed red raddle on his chest so that when he mounted a ewe he marked her. You can buy a special ram harness now with a block of dye in it, and as you can change the block to a different colour every week you can forecast the exact date of lambing by the colour.

Though nearly all the harvest is done now, except for sugar

beet (like Brian Aldridge has) and other roots, there is often a good spell of weather in November and if it comes in this month rather than October, it's known as St Martin's Little Summer because his day is on the 11th - and very nice it can be too!

You may remember last month I was telling you about birds and other creatures migrating. Well, people don't usually think of hares in this respect, but they do sort of migrate over a small area because in summer they spend most of their time in standing corn, and you don't see them much except at dawn and dusk when they come out to graze. Then when the corn is cut, they lie out in forms in stubble, or move into the woodland and only come out to feed at night. But as the root-crops develop, the hares move into them and feed, and lie-up there. By November when all the crops are about harvested they move out and lie on the bare ploughland, feeding on the new young corn as it comes up, and they do a lot of damage too - a great deal of nipping out of the hearts of young root-crops or market garden greens - so there are a lot of people they're not very popular with.

And rats too, which have been out in the fields all the summer living on grain and young birds and then on stubble, find life uncomfortable and food scarce by November, so there's an invasion of them into every farm about now. Of course, the farm-cat will kill some, and so will a good terrier, but the farmers have to do their bit too, so before the rats have had time to learn the geography properly you go out at night with a good dog, and a powerful flash lamp. You put on the lamp suddenly, and hope the dog will catch them before they get back to safety - oh yes, and you'd better remember to tuck your trousers in your socks if you don't want one to run up your leg.

And talking about being out in the dark, there's no use pretending as the nights isn't drawing in good and proper now. In fact, it's not more than another five weeks or so before we has the shortest day, 22 December, and that's when winter begins officially. Some folks find the nights drawin' in depressing, but I like to think of myself as a man for all seasons, and I find - being a countryman - something exciting about long, dark nights, they're so full of life, and you know, lying warm in bed isn't really the best way of hearing it going on.

The owls calling over the dark fields - there's music for you, good as any nightingale. Then there's a vixen yelling - an eerie sort of sound. And very often after it, the squeal of the rabbit as she's caught. It's all drama to my way of thinking, and what's more beautiful than a really angry winter sunset and the last of the rooks trailing home against it? But when I am out of a clear night in winter time, I feels as though I got the whole world to meself, except for the occasional noise I've been telling you about. Not a soul there, and everything still as it was that night last week when the new moon came up and there was 'the old moon in the new moon's arms'. And the brown owls was out on the hunt, too-hooing over the fields. And that's something I loves to hear. Some musical chap I met in The Bull one evening said as the owls calling sounded like some of the wood-wind in an orchestra. 'What's more', he went on, 'do you know as the tawny owl always make their calls in B Flat?' Well, of course I didn't. To me they was just the tawny owls as I like to hear.

And sometimes I hear the little owls yapping like dogs - 'Dutch Owls' some folks calls them - and there's always the screech of the barn-owl, and for my money he's the most handsome of the lot. Pity as they will go and kill theirselves diving at the headlights of cars, isn't it?

Where do you draw the line between mist and fog? I was out before it got light the other morning, and there had been just a catch of mist the night before that had made the moon look a bit sinister and ghostly, but instead of clearing when the dawn broke, it got thicker and I decided to go home for breakfast. That was what cut me down to size! I'd practically got the smell of Prue's bacon and eggs in me nostrils when it began to dawn on me that I didn't know whether I was a-comin' or going, 'cos by my calculations I should have been getting down the valley towards Arkwright Hall lake. Then I noticed I was going uphill instead of down! The mist had thickened instead of thinning, and although trees look as different as people when you see them clearly side by side, they are just like a platoon of soldiers in a fog. There weren't any familiar sounds either. I felt a proper fool, and was only thankful young Gordon couldn't see me - and I'd never have heard the last of it if anyone had told old Walter Gabriel!

Well, pulling myself together I set off determined to keep in a straight line because the wood isn't that big, and I was sure I could find my way when I came to the edge. Talk about convicts escaping from Dartmoor... I'd always heard they went in circles because one leg was shorter than the other. Well, mine must be too, because I kept going in circles - until at last I came to the path. Following it *down,* as I thought, I came to the stile at the top, with the letters T & PF, in a heart carved on it, when Prue and I got engaged all those years ago! Prue nearly tipped the bacon out of the pan with laughing when I got back and told her how hazed I was.

One of the things Prue and I are going to try to sell in a big way at the Garden Centre, is bird nest-boxes. So many folk come out of the town for plants, and seeds, and advice, that it makes me think that one of the nicest things they could have in their garden is a flock of wild birds. I don't mean *wild* wild birds, if you get me. I mean tame wild birds! Most folk have a bird-table and feed them all the winter, and that's a good start. But the real pleasure can come when the birds are feeding their youngsters in spring and summer, and the way to enjoy that properly is to persuade them to nest where you can see them. So a few weeks back, I got the wholesaler to supply me with a whole range of bird nest-boxes so that I could fix up a little exhibition, because you see they are things that don't want leaving to the last minute, since no wild bird in his senses will nest anywhere he hasn't had time to get familiar with. Well, I was a bit disappointed when the sample boxes arrived because a lot of them were horrible twee little things, but in the end I had a very good practical lot. One had a hole an inch and an eighth in diameter, big enough for great tits to squeeze through, and there was one with a hole only an inch and a sixteenth across, and that's just big enough for blue tits to get in but it will keep most other birds, like cheeky sparrows, out. You see it's critical what size the hole is, because if you choose right, you can help the pretty, gentle little birds, and the toughies - the starlings and sparrows - are quite capable of looking after themselves.

Anyhow I put up me sample range to give customers ideas, but as I was having a last look round, before shutting up for the night, would you believe it, I saw a tom tit go into one of the boxes I'd just put up. I was flabbergasted for a minute because it's months before the nesting season. And then I realised he was using my box as a nice warm roost to spend the winter in. By spring he'll have adopted it as his territory, and he'll court a hen, and persuade her to come and nest there - so that'll be one box we can't sell!

I was talking about the nights drawing in a little while back, well, when that happens in my opinion there's nowhere to beat your own fireside. Especially with a good log fire roaring half way up the chimney. We've always got big boughs snapping off in a storm, or an odd tree dying, and I always leave a bit of dead wood to encourage insects for woodpeckers and the wildlife that need grubs and beetles to live on, but Mr Woolley likes his woods to look tidy and well managed, so I clear up most of the stuff that would otherwise go rotten and get as much firewood for the house as Prue and I want.

To those who don't know better, a log is just a log. But not to us chaps who were brought up in the country. They say as there's no bad beer - but some is better than others. And it's just the same with firewood. Hawthorn and holly, for instance, make grand logs that burn very hot. Birch is all right, but it's soon gone. I often say it burns quicker than I can cut it up. But an old aunt of mine used to have a little ditty that said:

Birch and fir logs burn too fast,
Blaze up bright but do not last.
Make a fire of elder tree
Death within your house you'll see.
It is truly said
Hawthorn bakes the sweetest bread.
But ash green, or ash brown,
Is fit for a queen with a golden crown.

Like a good many of these old wives' tales, there's a lot in 'em, though don't believe all they say without trying it! Split birch logs do burn too fast, but big ones last well provided you don't split them. Some say that:

Elmwood burns like churchyard mould
E'en the very flames are cold.

But I've had grand elm that's seasoned for a year, though it isn't really safe to keep now, because of the Dutch elm disease and the beetles that come out and infect other elms.

So if anyone offers you a load of logs, make sure what tree they come from. Nothing, absolutely nothing, beats fruit tree wood, and with the modern craze for grubbing out apple orchards you can sometimes get a load of apple logs. Apple, or pear, or cherry, will scent the whole house so you know it's home, the moment you open the front door. I'd rather have an old apple tree butt for my Yuletide log than a whole case of champagne - and it won't be long before it's Christmas now, will it, so you'd better start getting ready for it, hadn't you?

December

When icicles hang by the wall
And Dick the shepherd blows his nail,
And Tom bears logs into the hall,
And milk comes frozen home in pail,
Then nightly sings the staring owl...

It's often a dull, dank month, isn't it? With the shortest day and longest night in it. The hips and haws have shrivelled, the moles have dug a bit deeper after the worms that have gone down to avoid the frost, fish can die if there's ice, not because of the cold but from lack of oxygen and even shy birds will come near your house for food. But do you know, although we complain about our winters, I reckon they were much worse years ago. Prue and I came across a passage in that old book I was telling you about which bears this out, because it said two hundred or so years ago: 'The frost was so severe the street lamps couldn't be lit on account of the oil being frozen; many people were found frozen to death in the fields and roads, and thousands of birds were picked up dead' and even if we do grumble now, the ivy's green, the robins are singing, there's mistletoe on the old hawthorns and old apple trees, the holly bushes have bright shining leaves and clusters of red berries, and there'll be carol singers, and Christmas before long, so why shouldn't we be cheerful, eh?

Do you know talking of that, and telling you last month about the old stile where Prue and I carved our initials when we were courting, has reminded me that about that time, I remembered a line or two of a poem I'd read at school, by Tennyson I think it was - anyroad I used to say them to Prue:

Their meetings made December June,
Their every parting was to die.

And it's good isn't it, that after all these years, we should still be together, and happy, even if we didn't ever have any children of our own - though Peter and Johnnie as we fostered have been good boys to us and we're a bit sad now as Peter's moved off to live in Borchester on his own - even if on his own means with his girl friend!

A few months ago I was talking to you about robins singing in December, well, we've got our 'back-door' robin at last. I says 'at last' because he's taken a fine old time to make up his mind as our bit of garden wouldn't be a bad place to be of a wintertime. Ever since October he's been casting his bright eye on us from the hazel coppice just across the lane, and singing his rather sad autumn song. Then come that hard, bright spell end of last month, and over the lane he came, straight to Prue's bird-table where he saw off a couple of starlings quick as you please, and now first thing in the morning his lordship stands fat as a red billiard ball on the kitchen window-sill, tapping with his beak on the glass as if to say: 'Hey, you lot in there, how long's a feller got to wait for his breakfast?'

I reckon he was one of the brood that was hatched out from a nest inside a flower-pot as I'd left lying on its side, back of the garden shed last spring. We've got our own special thrush too. Properly adopted us he has, but of all our garden birds he's the most nervous. I've even seen him fly off the bird-table at the sight of a little wren a quarter his size. And of course, there's all the tits, there's nothing timid about them!

Oh, yes, garden birds - even those cocky little bullies, the sparrows - are a joy to have about, and well worth the slice of housekeeping money as my Prue never stops spending on them. Not that water costs anything, and that's one thing some folks often forgets to put out for them when their natural supplies is all frozen over - and it's so easy, isn't it? And it's a good time to start feeding them properly so that if really hard weather comes in January and February, they will already have learned where to come.

The other day I saw Martha Woodford was already making a tit-cake. Do you know about that? Well, you get any odd bits of fat, and melt it thoroughly till it's all liquid, and pour it over a basinful of any scraps that are going - crumbs, bacon rind, apple peel, monkey-nuts, dog-biscuit, that kind of thing. Then you wait till the fat hardens into a sort of cake, then tip it out and hang the whole thing up outside, and the birds will soon get at it without bits being dropped on the ground and being pinched by the mice - besides this way you can enjoy watching them getting their meal while knowing they're well out of the reach of cats.

And while I'm on about the birds in our garden, let me tell you about nest-boxes - not the ones I was on about in the Garden Centre but the ones I put up for the birds last year and had a fair bit of luck with - two lots of blue tits, a pair of great tits, and even a pair of cole tits. Lovely little birds all of them and all useful about the garden for the insects they caught and fed their fledglings on.

But the box that gave me most pleasure wasn't the ordinary sort with an entrance hole about as big as an old-fashioned penny. No - it was what bird watchers call an open-fronted box, about nine inches high with a sloping roof, and an entrance under the eaves about two inches square. It hung just under the big bough of the old apple tree opposite the kitchen window - and a pair of spotted flycatchers reared a brood there. Prue and me had endless pleasure while we was having our meals watching the old birds bring thousands and thousands of flies for their hungry brood to feed on.

He who shall hurt the little wren
Shall never be loved by men.

Now you might think getting on for Christmas is a funny time to be talking about flycatchers which flew off to sunny Africa in the autumn, but although they've gone - we're still getting pleasure from that box! Instead of flycatchers, the wrens are using it now. Not to nest in, of course, but to sleep in. Every evening just as it's getting dusk - while Prue and me are having our tea, a wren flies up and pops into the box. And the moment he disappears, he's followed by another, and another, and another, and we count fourteen or fifteen piling in. Of course wrens are almost the smallest birds we have. But even so, as I told you before, when we were talking about January I think it was, they cram so many in that box that there must be a bit of a fug - and that's the idea of course, to keep warm.

You may remember as I'm not very keen on holidays but Prue likes them so some years back we decided as we'd go on a coach trip to Scotland, and that made a change from the road to Penny Hassett, I can tell you. One day we found ourselves looking at the old Forth Bridge, y'know the one as carries the railway and which they never stops painting, year in, year out. I asked a chap as was standing beside me how the painters managed to get on with it on the really hard days of winter in a north-easterly with maybe snow into the bargain.

'Oh,' he said, 'they goes inside.' 'Inside?' I said, 'inside where?' 'Inside the big steel tubes as the bridge is built from,' said the chap. 'What you don't see has got to be painted just the same as what you do see. That's the cold weather work.'

And come to think of it, much the same goes for farmers, once the potatoes and the sugar beet's lifted, the land ploughed, and the winter wheat sown. There's never any shortage of under-cover work in the barns and farm outbuildings, I can tell you. But when you comes to open-air work around this time of the year, it's the hedges as takes priority. It's the time for trimming and tidying up the loose ends, and there's few things to my way of thinking as looks better than a winter-trimmed hedge 'short back and sides', with the bonfires of the loose-ends crackling and smoking all along the line - and the scent of that smoke - lovely of a winter's afternoon!

Mind you, it's sad to me that it's not so often as you see a properly 'laid' hedge these days, the sapling growth bent around strong stakes, and the top of the hedge woven tight with rods what the hedge-layers calls 'hethers'. I reckon, saving here and there in the countryside, the craft of hedge-laying takes too much time and trouble for folk these days. Though when you *do* see one - a real delight to the eye it is.

Around full-moon at this time of year, you'd be surprised what a lot of birds you can see feeding in the dead of night. There's a field of young grass a good quarter of a mile from Arkwright Hall lake, for instance, and I heard a lovely, sizzling sort of conversation going on down there last full-moon. The sort of chatter you hear outside the village hall when the Womens' Institute is meeting. So I sneaked down to see what it was, and I should think there were a couple of hundred wild duck, dibbling around and each telling his neighbour when he found a tasty grub.

And there was a flock of peewits on a ploughed field next to it, running round to pick up worms and leatherjackets, flying and swooping over the rest of the flock, singing that wild, mournful tune that only plover know.

And often I notice when the moon's very bright, that those wild duck, and plover, and wading birds hunch up in sleep all day, looking proper drowsy and uninteresting. Like us they can't burn their candle at both ends, you see!

But I was rewarded the other night, because a catch of frost had pulled white gloves over every twig and branch, so the whole countryside had the festive look and spirit before its time.

But one night last week I got a surprise when I come home a bit late from The Bull. I was just going up our garden path when my foot knocked against something soft. Well, perhaps I should say it felt kind of solid, with a soft case. So I bent down to have a look what it was, and there, closed up as tight as a clenched fist, was a smallish hedgehog. Hedgehogs ought to be hibernating by now, and that was what surprised me, and when I bent down to move him to somewhere safer, I was more surprised still. Not only was he a smallish hedgehog, but he was very light too. And I reckoned he was the victim of that dry summer we had, and that he'll remember it as long as he lives, which doesn't look like being long. You see, hedgehogs eat a tremendous amount of earth-worms - and worms had to dig so deep to find moist soil that there were hardly any on the surface for the hedgehogs. All through the autumn, I've seen young hedgehogs - or urchins, as we call them - working all hours to get enough to live on. In normal years by about the end of October, they put on thick layers of fat. Then when the cold weather comes, they roll into a ball under an eiderdown of warm leaves and sleep away the winter. But they can only survive if they have done themselves well enough to live off their fat till spring, and the poor little fellow I nearly trod on last night simply hadn't got enough fat, so he's got to go on finding food when he really should be comfortably wrapped up and asleep. And if we get a cold spell, a really cold spell, he won't be able to find the food and he won't have enought fat to carry him through without it, so I felt real sorry for him.

I was talking to a chap in The Bull the other day who'd come out of the town and who worked in a factory. He was fed-up with the foreman, and the clock punchin', but above all he was fed-up with havin' to do exactly the same job day after day. He was sayin' how wonderful it would be to work on a farm in the peace and quiet of the countryside.

Well, the grass is always greener on the other side of the fence! Have you ever wondered what it must feel like to drive your tractor into a hundred acre field, perhaps half a mile long and more than a quarter of a mile across? You start on Monday morning, ploughing a furrow half a mile long. And when you get to the end of it, you turn round and plough the next one, half a mile back. And even if you've got a modern plough and tractor powerful enough to turn four or even five furrows at a time, you still have to crawl up the field at walking pace and then crawl back from Monday morning right on till Saturday night, so that next week you can start all over again in the next field. That's not only a repetitive job, it's pretty lonely too. Nobody to talk to from morning to night - and not much peace and quiet either, with the roar of a tractor in your ears and the vibration shimmering up your spine!

And yet for all that, that chap in the pub was right, you know. Workin' on the land may be as repetitive as most jobs - and far less comfortable - but it's much more satisfying! Everyone in the village can see whether you're any good at it or not! A furrow fading in the skyline without a kink or a twist in it is an achievement to be proud of. And a field of furrows with never a clump of stubble that's not been buried, commands everyone's respect when you go in the local at night.

And while you're harrowing and sowing the corn, you get to know every rabbit, and hare, and pheasant, and peewit that feeds on the land as well as you do the hens in the backyard at home. They've nothing to fear from mechanical implements, so every tractor driver can enjoy the wildlife around him, and see dramas going on that are never written about in books.

And by harvest next year, when the corn's been sown, and grown, and ripened, the chap who's tended it for twelve months has done something *creative* that makes him love the countryside, however boring and uncomfortable it may sometimes be.

Now one of the big changes that has come to living in the country in my time has been the electricity. That's really taken a lot of the irk out of work! Mother used to mess about for well nigh an hour every morning trimming paraffin lamps, or we couldn't see across the kitchen at night. And we couldn't boil a kettle for a cup of tea in the morning until we'd got the coal fire in the kitchen grate kindled. Now we just switch on an electric kettle! But it's not everybody likes all these innovations. Some say that pylons across the skyline spoil the view, though I must admit that I find a quick cuppa on a cold morning warms my heart better than the view!

Another thing that's changed a lot in my time has been the

mail. You all knows about our post office bus which Harry Booker drives - postal service and fare-paying passengers combined. Well, it was Mr Adamson's idea that I should go round with Harry and deliver the Christmas parcels for some of the old folks that live round about. And this started me thinking about the post service in Ambridge when I was a bit of a boy. The mail used to arrive early in the morning at Hollerton Junction, and around seven o'clock a chap, name of Amos Andrews, used to pick it up and do the round of the villages nearby. He went clop-clopping along in his pony and trap, dropping the letters and that for each village at what used to pass for the village post-office in them days. Here in Ambridge an old couple called Sarah and Simeon Brent used to run a little shop across the Green from The Bull, and Simeon - well, he was postmaster, and very proud of it too.

Now when he'd sorted out the 'running-order' of the mail as you might say, he'd take the letters on foot to every farm or cottage in the parish, and as a lad I'd go with him, and we'd stop and gather a few mushrooms, or something from the hedges, and once one spring what we ought not to a-done - a clutch of fresh-laid moorhens' eggs. Oh, but they was lovely, fried with a bit of bacon for breakfast - I can remember them still.

We're coming up towards the season of Good Cheer now - and it's a wonderful time for stealing. Fowl thieves come round to scrump a bird for the table or a few to sell for beer-money and if they're local they choose a night when there's a function on at the village hall or a dance, or a Young Farmers 'do' the owner is likely to be at. Whereas strangers go by where the lights are, and pick a night when there's something special on the telly which is a much safer time than later when everyone respectable is likely to be in bed.

You might be surprised at the mad rush there's been for Christmas trees at the Garden Centre this year and it nearly ended in disaster. You see, we've got an acre of young spruce growing in the nursery, so we dug up most of the thinnings about a fortnight ago to sell for Christmas. They have been going like hot cakes because they were beautiful young trees, and we don't scald the roots, like some do. That means that if folk put them in a tub of moist sand and keep it moist, they can plant the trees when Christmas is over and have a good chance of 'em growing in the garden. Anyhow we miscalculated the number we wanted and didn't bring in nearly enough, so I slipped off down to the nursery after I'd finished work to dig up some more. Dusk was just fading into dark, and I half noticed a van in the road with its headlights off. But thinking it was a courting couple, I took no notice and hurried on to get the trees while I could more or less see what I was about. There wasn't a sound, and there wasn't a movement, but having been a keeper so long, I have a sort of sixth sense which seems to tell me when strangers are around. So I froze still and waited, knowing that practice had taught me to stay still longer than most, and that that unprofessional ass couldn't stand the strain. He coughed! So I made a dive in that direction, and hearing me coming, he scuffled off through the plantation.

Of course, I knew the lie of the land better than he did, so I nipped round to try and head him off. If he'd gone straight for the van I'd have had him, but he must have lost his way and come out at a thick bit of hedge. He was in such a panic that he dived straight through, prickles and all. And I reckon the scratching he got would do more good than any fine if I'd managed to catch him and summon him for stealing our trees. And I got a bonus too, because I only had to carry off the trees he'd dug up instead of digging them up myself!

It's a funny thing but I've noticed, come December, so many folks says to other folks: 'You going away for Christmas?' Rather like in summertime: 'Had your holdiays, yet?' Going *away* for Christmas! Not as I'm blaming some folks whose idea of Christmas is to get all cosied up in some warm hotel with everything laid on, and someone else to do the cooking. Good luck to them I say, but to my way of thinking the real heart of Christmas is staying at home, specially if you live in a place like Ambridge. Fancy wanting to 'go away' from the Christmas pudding you've helped to stir, and the roast turkey you'd known afore it was even a gobbler in that farmyard over Netherbourne way. Oh, yes, there's still a few country farmers - or farmers' wives - as rears three or four dozen birds for their regular customers. And of course, it's sad when you passes a farmyard mid-December, all filled up with red wattles and a 'gobble-gobble-gobble', only to know as the next time you goes by there's only silence, and a fine twelve-pounder hanging ready for the oven in your larder.

But that's the way of it in a real country Christmas. So many shared things - the pub raffles, and the Christmas cards as Sid and Polly have got hanging up in The Bull. The Christmas whist-drives and dances in the village hall, and the holly-berries bright in the cottage gardens. Yes, I know I'm old-fashioned, but I wouldn't 'go away for Christmas' from Ambridge and my friends, and neighbours, for all the tea in China!

Did you know that holly is also called Christ's Thorn, and that when a robin plucked a thorn from Christ's brow the blood stained his breast red? And that mistletoe is only effective for kissing under if the man plucks a berry for each kiss - and when all the berries are gone you're too late? And that you should put it up on 21 December so it will ward off damage by frost? Did you know all that? Did you?

But have you noticed how still it is at Christmas? You can hear the barking of some farm dog far, far away, and a tawny owl in the distance, but the most wonderful sound of all coming across the still countryside is the church bells and the carols of the Christmas Eve midnight service. And they used to say that on Christmas Eve the cattle kneel down in their stalls, the bees sing in their hives, and that bread baked that day will never go mouldy.

Then on Boxing Day, there's always a shoot which in the good old days was for the tenants and farmers, and even farm labourers went rabiting with ferrets and some went pike fishing. And the other thing is the Boxing Day Meet, which is the meet of the year, but of course the holiday season is no holiday for keepers or farmers - stock and pigs has to be fed, cows milked, horses exercised, and sheep folded, just like any other day of the year.

And now you've come round with me nearly to New Year's Day and the start of another year, and I shall be off with our little band of bell-ringers up into the belfry of our church to ring in the New Year, and all the hope it brings for our future.